## "WE ARE GOING TO FORM A SECRET ORDER, SORT OF AN AUXILIARY TO THE AGAINST TAFFY SINCLAIR CLUB."

"What for?" I asked. I couldn't see what forming a secret club had to do with Taffy Sinclair and her you-know-whats.

"The purpose of the secret order," Beth went on, giving me a frown that had to mean "Shut up," "is to increase our bustlines faster than Taffy."

# THE AGAINST
# TAFFY SINCLAIR
# CLUB

Betsy Haynes

A BANTAM SKYLARK BOOK®
TORONTO · NEW YORK · LONDON · SYDNEY · AUCKLAND

This edition contains the complete text
of the original hardcover edition.
NOT ONE WORD HAS BEEN OMITTED.

RL 4, IL age 9 and up

THE AGAINST TAFFY SINCLAIR CLUB
A Bantam Book / published by arrangement with
Thomas Nelson Inc.

PRINTING HISTORY
Thomas Nelson edition published November 1976
Bantam Skylark edition / February 1981
8 printings through September 1988

*For my daughter Stephanie*
*with love*

# 1

Friday is Wretched-Mess Day. That's the day I clean my room. Mom picked Friday because she said that my room ought to look nice for the weekend just in case we have any company, which we sometimes do. Mostly I keep my door closed so I can have some privacy, but I have to admit that when it's open my entire wretched mess is visible from the living-room sofa, and that is where company usually sits.

This particular Wretched-Mess Day Mom went into a fit. I guess what set her off was a call she got about a bill being overdue, added to the fact that my father had missed another support payment. Anyway, before she left our apartment for work she tore around like Roadrunner screaming that I had to clean out all the garbage under my bed. You'd have thought the health department was on its way out to quarantine the apartment from the way she carried

1

on. And I really resented her calling my things garbage. It's all good stuff. I just don't have any other place to put it.

At first I was glad that I had cleaned out under my bed. I found some things that I'd been looking for for a while. There was an overdue book under there that I had forgotten to return to the school library before summer vacation started, and the sombrero my friend Melanie Edwards brought me from Tijuana, and the blue ribbon I won last spring for being the best speller in the fourth grade, not to mention one red sneaker, one green knee sock, my Girl Scout canteen, and my brown-and-gold-plaid skirt.

There was also my notebook from the Against Taffy Sinclair Club, of which I am the president. Taffy Sinclair and I hate each other just about as much as any two people can, which is why I have this club. My four best friends belong. We don't really do much in our club except talk about Taffy and how she carries on in front of the boys, batting her eyelashes and dropping things all the time so that she can bend over and show her underpants. Just before school was out for the summer we started collecting five cents dues every week so we could send her cards like the one that said, "You must have been a beautiful baby, but Baby, look at you now!" and which had a picture of King Kong on the inside. Once we ordered a free sample of a new kind of sanitary napkin sent to her, but we don't know if she ever got it.

Taffy doesn't have a club. She doesn't even have very many friends, because she's stuck up and snotty and thinks she's the most gorgeous creature in the world. Hardly anyone wants to have anything to do with her, except maybe Mona Vaughn. Mona has a huge nose and buck teeth and is just about as ugly as Taffy Sinclair is pretty. She has some friends of her own, but every so often she follows Taffy around for a few days as if she thought some of Taffy's looks would rub off on her. It never lasts long, though, because Taffy is just as snotty to Mona as she is to everyone else.

You can tell that Taffy's a really horrible person by the things she does. Take, for instance, what she did on the last day of school. I nearly died. I walked into the fourth-grade room and someone had written on the blackboard, "Jana Morgan has B.O." I knew who had done it. It had to be Taffy Sinclair.

As I said before, I was pretty glad to find all of those things under my bed. It was what I pulled out last that made that Wretched-Mess Day extra wretched. To the casual observer, it was just an ordinary shoe box. Well, it wasn't really a shoe box. It was a boot box. I picked it because it was bigger than any of my shoe boxes. In it I keep all the letters I've ever gotten from my father since he and my mother were divorced when I was three. There are only four, which isn't very many for practically my whole lifetime. Of course it isn't all his fault that he doesn't write more often. He changes jobs and moves around a lot, and that can really keep a person busy.

Mom doesn't know that I've saved the letters. I don't suppose she'd mind. After all, she's always telling me what a great person my father is and how on the night they met he asked her to dance and they kept on dancing until after midnight, and

3

things like that. I haven't told her about my boot box because it's just something I sort of want to keep private.

Letters aren't the only things I keep in that box. I guess you'd call the other things souvenirs. I don't have very many, at least not very many different kinds of things. I have a whole bunch of envelopes that my support-payment checks came in. I dug them out of the trash, so a couple of them are messed up with coffee grounds and stuff. They're all alike, though, so I stopped collecting them.

Another thing I keep there is a picture. It was taken last Christmas and shows me in front of a tree with all my presents. I'm holding a doll that my father sent me. He doesn't usually send me regular presents. Mostly he just adds a little extra to that month's check. Mom made some remark about me taking the doll with me on my next date and then packed it away for me to give to my little girl someday. I thought that was a funny thing to say since I was only ten then and I didn't go on dates, but I didn't play with dolls anymore either.

Anyway, I sat there staring at that box for a long time, knowing that I shouldn't open it. It's funny how sometimes the more you know you shouldn't do something the more you have to do it. It's sort of like . . . well, you can't help yourself. My hands were shaking so hard that I almost couldn't get the lid off. But I did, and there on top was That Letter—That Letter that had ruined my entire summer.

I picked it up and opened the envelope just as if I didn't know what was in it. There it was, the Easter card with the dumb pink duck on the front, that dumb pink duck with the stupid grin on its face

4

carrying a basket of weird-looking eggs. I never saw such a dumb pink duck. Inside the card was a piece of paper, which I let fall into my lap. It was such a tiny piece of paper that it's really a compliment to call it a letter.

I didn't look at it. I didn't have to. I knew all the words by heart. All it said was, "Dear Jana, Sometime this summer I am going west for a two-week vacation. Would you like to come with me? I would like that very much. Love, Your Father."

Thank goodness the phone rang just as I was about to cry, which would have been a silly thing to do. I dropped that dumb pink duck right on his nose and ran into the living room to answer the phone.

It was Beth Barry, my best friend. "Jana!" she shouted, nearly knocking out my ear. "She's back!"

"Who's back?"

"Taffy Sinclair, who else?"

"What's so unreal about that? School starts next week," I said. Beth gets kind of carried away sometimes. Taffy had been gone all summer, but there was nothing strange about her coming back in time for school.

"Wait until you see her. You won't believe it. I think we'd better call the club into emergency session."

"Did she suddenly get a case of the uglies?" I asked hopefully. "Did all her beautiful blond hair fall out? Did those great big basset-hound eyes swell shut? Did . . ."

"Shut up, you idiot. I hate to tell you, but it's nothing like that. In fact, it's sort of the reverse."

Neither one of us said anything for a minute. I couldn't imagine Taffy Sinclair getting any prettier, but I had to know.

5

"Well?" I said.

"Sit down," said Beth.

I did.

"Well?" I said again.

"Okay, here goes. Taffy Sinclair has you-know-whats!"

"Oh, no," I groaned. It was almost too much to stand. What more could one girl have? I must have groaned for a full five minutes before I pulled myself together. "What good would an emergency session of the club do?"

"I have a plan."

"What kind of plan?"

"I can't tell you over the phone," Beth whispered dramatically. "But it just may be the greatest plan you ever heard."

"I doubt that," I snickered. "But anything is worth a try. Call everyone and tell them to be over here in forty-five minutes."

After I hung up I hurried back into my room to finish cleaning up my wretched mess before my friends came over. There was my boot box right where I had left it. I picked up the letter off the floor and tossed it back into the box. Then I slammed on the lid and shoved it under the bed again. This wasn't the time to worry about the letter.

I went to the dressing-table mirror and looked at my front. I turned sideways very slowly and stared as hard as I could, but there wasn't the slightest sign of any you-know-whats. Our teacher was always raving about good posture, so I stood up extra straight, but that didn't do any good either.

I couldn't help but wonder what it was like to have you-know-whats. Could you see your shoes when you were standing up? I looked down. Boy, could I see mine! How could you sleep on your stomach? I always sleep on my stomach. I wouldn't want to give that up. I wondered if Taffy Sinclair was still sleeping on her stomach. It would sure serve her right if she wasn't.

# 2

---

Beth was there in half an hour. I hadn't even finished cleaning up my wretched mess. She was carrying her Against Taffy Sinclair Club notebook as if it were a time bomb. Then I noticed a magazine stuck in it and tried to see what it was, but she jerked the notebook away and sat on it so that I couldn't see it. You'd have thought she was a spy or something.

Melanie Edwards got there next. As usual, she brought a sack of brownies. I think her mother must make brownies twenty-four hours a day. I think Melanie must eat them just about that often, too. Mom says she'll probably lose some of her weight when she gets to be a teenager. I hope so because right now the boys don't talk to her very much.

Christie Winchell came in a couple of minutes later. Christie is a mathematical genius, and I've always wondered if it has anything to do with the fact that her mother is principal of our school. Everyone was there except Katie Shannon, who had to stay home and help get things ready for her mother's encounter-group meeting. Katie is the radical feminist of our group. Don't get me wrong. We're all into the women's movement, but Katie is in really deep.

There is just one chair in my room, the one at my desk, so everybody plopped down on the floor. I tried to look at each girl's front when she came in. I tried to be casual so that no one would know what I was looking at, but that was very hard to do. Then I made a mistake and looked at Beth's front. She was looking at mine. We caught each other at exactly the same moment, and I could feel my ears getting red. I folded my arms across my front, and Beth did, too, but not before I could see that she didn't have any you-know-whats either.

I decided to start the meeting before I got any more depressed, and I pounded Mom's hammer on the radiator a couple of times for attention since we didn't have a real gavel.

"This emergency meeting of the Against Taffy Sinclair Club will come to order."

Everyone stopped talking and sat still except for Melanie, who was crawling around the room passing out her brownies.

"Taffy Sinclair is back in town from her summer vacation. Beth saw her and told me that we have a new crisis."

"What kind of crisis?" Melanie asked.

"Taffy Sinclair has you-know-whats!"

I might as well have announced that Mark Twain Elementary was being turned into an all-girls school. There was a horrified look on every

9

face, but no one said a word. Instead, they all slouched forward at the same time, letting their blouses hang loose so they would hide their chests. The Radio City Music Hall Rockettes couldn't have done it with more precision timing.

"I'll bet the boys will really like her now," said Christie.

Everybody giggled. It sort of broke the tension, and we all started squirming around, secretly trying to look at each other's fronts out of the corners of our eyes.

I banged the hammer on the radiator again.

"Beth has a plan," I shouted. That brought everybody to attention.

Beth cleared her throat and then stood up, which really wasn't necessary since there were only four of us in the room and we could all see her just fine.

"Everybody raise your right hand and solemnly swear that no one outside this room will ever know what we're going to do," she whispered hoarsely.

I looked at Christie and shrugged, and she shrugged back. Then we two slowly raised our right hands. So did Melanie.

"We are going to form a secret order, sort of an auxiliary to the Against Taffy Sinclair Club."

"What for?" I asked. I couldn't see what forming a secret club had to do with Taffy Sinclair and her you-know-whats.

"The purpose of the secret order," Beth went on, giving me a frown that had to mean "Shut up," "is to increase our bustlines faster than Taffy."

"How can we do that?" asked Christie. "Are you some kind of magician? Besides, Taffy already has a head start."

10

"I'm no magician," said Beth. "But Milo Venus is!"

"Who's Milo Venus?" I asked.

Beth whipped the magazine out of her Against Taffy Sinclair Club notebook. It was an issue of *Redbook,* which my mother also gets. I usually look through it, and I didn't remember seeing anything about any magician who could do a thing like that.

"Right here on page two hundred and three," Beth said. She pointed triumphantly at a full-page advertisement with a big picture of a very shapely blonde in it, plus a bunch of before and after pictures. "It says, 'Milo Venus is the world's foremost bustline developer.' "

"Wow! Look at her," said Melanie. " 'I increased my bustline from thirty-six to a full forty inches in just five weeks with the fantastic Milo Venus Developer,' " she read.

"How does it work?" asked Christie.

"I'm not sure," Beth said. "All it says here is, 'It employs special techniques safely and effectively' and so on and so on. But it does have a money-back guarantee if you don't get results in two weeks."

"Money," I said. "We don't have any money. How much does it cost, anyway?"

"Nineteen ninety-five," Beth said sort of sheepishly.

"Nineteen *dollars,* and ninety-five cents!" Melanie shrieked.

"That's not so much," said Beth. "We can have weekly dues."

"We already pay five cents to the Against Taffy Sinclair Club," I said.

"Well, if we each added another five cents to that and put it all in the secret-order treasury, we would have a total of fifty cents a week," said Beth.

Christie began scribbling in her notebook.

"At that rate it would take . . . um . . . forty weeks to raise the money," she said. "We can't wait that long."

"We can walk dogs or wash cars or something," said Beth. "Everybody think hard between now and next Friday. We'll have another meeting then."

"Okay, but what are we going to call our secret order?" I asked.

"I've already thought of that," said Beth. "I think we should have sort of a code name. Then we can talk about it and it will drive Taffy wild trying to figure out what it means."

"Great," I said. "But what kind of code name can we use?"

"Lambda Rho," Beth said.

"Lamb the what?" said Christie, screwing up her face.

"Lambda Rho," Beth repeated. "Those are the Greek letters for *l* and *r*. My sister is in a sorority at college and they call practically everything by Greek letters. It's the weirdest thing you ever heard."

"Hey, that's neat," said Melanie. "But what do the *l* and *r* stand for?"

Beth swallowed and looked embarrassed. "Little raisins," she said softly.

There was a lot more giggling and squirming, but everybody finally agreed that Lambda Rho was a great name and that it would drive Taffy up a tree trying to figure it out.

After everybody left, the phone rang. It was Katie.

12

"Sorry I couldn't make the meeting. Beth said it was really important. Some kind of crisis."

"Taffy Sinclair's back in town, and she's got you-know-whats."

"Huh?"

"I said, Taffy Sinclair's back, and she's got you-know-whats."

"Do you mean breasts?" Katie asked, sounding really disgusted.

"Yeah," I answered awkwardly.

"Then *say* breasts!" she shrieked. "That's what's the matter with women today. They can't face reality. They're not 'you-know-whats.' They're breasts."

"Okay. Okay. Taffy Sinclair has . . . breasts. Are you satisfied?"

"So who needs them? Men only point them out as a sign of our inferiority."

I couldn't help snickering. The day that I would feel inferior because I had a gorgeous figure would be some freaky day. But I didn't say it out loud. It would have only made her madder.

"Even Gloria Steinem has breasts," I offered hopefully.

Katie made a horrible snorting noise and lapsed into silence.

I stood it as long as I could and then plunged in again. "Well, look at it this way. It's a step toward becoming a genuine, bona fide bra burner. I mean, in order to burn one, you've got to own one. Right?"

I could hear her laughing at the other end of the line, and although she wouldn't agree to go along with the plan for another fifteen minutes, I knew that I had her. By the end of the conversation she actually said that the whole idea was far out.

After we hung up, I got two pairs of rolled-up socks out of my bureau drawer and stuck them under my blouse. Then I sauntered up to the mirror, turned sideways, and surveyed my shape.

"Your money back if you don't get results in two weeks," I whispered to the curvaceous female staring out at me.

# 3

The first day of school was a disaster. I knew it would be the minute I opened one eye and saw Mom rummaging around in my closet. I knew what she was doing. She was looking for the icky purple dress that she had bought for me to wear on the first day of school. I hated it the minute I saw it. It had a white collar and matching tights and looked like something a first grader would wear. Worst of all, the top was made out of some kind of stretchy material that's all puckery and sewn with elastic thread. It fit so tightly across my front that I almost couldn't breathe. The whole world would be able to tell at a glance how flat-chested I was.

I had hidden it in the back of my closet, hoping that Mom would forget all about it, but of course she didn't. I kept telling her that all my friends were wearing jeans and T-shirts. She kept telling me that

15

I should be an individual, and besides, that the dress had cost a fortune. She finally hit the ceiling when I told her I thought that she had been gypped.

I walked all the way to school holding my notebook across my front. Nobody said anything about my icky purple dress. My friends are all too polite for that. But I could tell that they didn't like it, either.

It was great to get back to school and see a lot of kids that I hadn't seen all summer. Sally Schmidt had been to Europe, and Clarence Marshall had his arm in a cast. Clarence Marshall is a real drip. He is always doing weird things, like squirting the water fountain all over everybody. I never could stand him, but I was sorry that he broke his arm.

I kept looking around the school ground for Taffy Sinclair. It was almost time for the bell and she was nowhere to be seen. I wondered if she was planning to be late so that she could make a grand entrance.

Then I saw her. I almost *died.* She was crossing the street and coming toward school in an icky purple dress just like mine. It had the same white collar and the same matching tights, and the front was made of that tight, stretchy stuff, just like mine. Worst of all, there wasn't any doubt that she had breasts.

My heart sank into my shoes. I clutched my notebook against my front. My arms were already getting numb from holding it there so long, but I didn't care. Gangrene could set in before I'd move that notebook.

If looks could kill, I would have been dead the instant Taffy Sinclair spotted me. Well, one thing was certain. I would never wear that icky purple dress again, no matter how much it had cost!

You would have thought that those were enough troubles for one day. I sure thought so, anyway. But that was before the bell rang and I saw my new fifth-grade teacher.

Beth and Melanie and Christie and Katie and I had all gotten seats next to each other on the right side of the room and were talking so hard that we didn't hear *him* come in.

His name was Mr. Neal, and he was the dreamiest man I'd ever seen in my whole life. He had wavy brown hair and blue eyes. They must have been the bluest eyes in the whole world. They were kind, too. You could tell that he was kind and sensitive, the sort of person you'd want to tell your troubles to.

It was plain to see that my friends felt the same way about Mr. Neal as I did. Melanie was staring at him so hard that her mouth was open. I thought about poking her and telling her to close it. I would have died if he had caught me doing something like that.

Naturally Taffy Sinclair was sitting in the front row. She was so close to him that she could have reached out and touched his desk. She kept looking at me over her shoulder. Gloating. I hated her more than ever.

Then he started talking about the subjects we would be studying and what he hoped we would accomplish during the year. How on earth could I do schoolwork with someone like that in the same room? What would I do when he called on me or sent me to the blackboard? Good grief! What if I had

17

to go to the bathroom? How could I possibly raise my hand and ask to leave the room? He would know where I was going. I would be so embarrassed that I'd die.

Next he made a big speech about how important it was for students and teachers to be able to communicate with each other. He said that we should always come to him if we had any problems or difficulties.

I always had difficulties with history. It was my worst subject. I just couldn't memorize all those stupid dates. I didn't see why they were so important anyway. Maybe I'd go to him about history. No. I'd feel dumb and self-conscious.

Then I got this great idea. Math had always been my best subject. I'd fake not understanding a problem. Then he would sit beside me under the giant copper beech tree in front of the school, and while everybody watched he would patiently explain it to me. Then I would look up at him and tell him how grateful I was and that now I understood. Then I would work all the problems in just about a split second and he would tell me how proud of me he was and how glad he was that I was in his class.

"Pssst. Pssst. Jana. It's your turn."

I looked around to see the whole class and Mr. Neal staring straight at me. I thought I'd die. While I had been dreaming about sitting under the copper beech tree with him, the rest of the class had been doing something else. Now it was my turn, and I didn't know what to do.

"Stand up and give your name, please," said Mr. Neal. There was a trace of irritation in his voice.

I stood up very slowly. My ears were so hot that

I thought any minute they would melt and drip down my shoulders.

"Jana Morgan," I said in a quivery voice about three octaves higher than usual. Then I realized that I didn't have my notebook over my front. Everybody was still looking at me. Me and my flat front. I couldn't have sat down any faster if the floor had opened up underneath me.

The rest of the day went pretty smoothly. When the dismissal bell finally rang, Beth and Melanie and Katie and Christie and I headed for the door in a cluster. Mr. Neal was standing there saying good-bye to everybody as they left. We all exchanged knowing glances as we watched Taffy Sinclair leaving just ahead of us.

"Watch her faint so that he has to catch her," said Katie.

Taffy moved slowly toward the crowded doorway. With each step she edged a little closer to the side where Mr. Neal stood. Finally she was right beside him. I didn't understand at first when I saw her put her hand on her hip. Then I realized that she had done it so that her elbow would stick out. I swallowed hard as I saw her elbow brush against his sleeve as she walked by. That was bad enough, but then she turned around and looked at me. She might as well have been carrying a neon sign and said, *I touched him.*

I couldn't let her get away with a thing like that.

"I just can't wait until the next meeting of Lambda Rho," I blurted out.

That stopped her cold. Somebody was jabbing me in the side, but I ignored it and just enjoyed the look on Taffy's face. You would have thought that I

19

had just been named Miss America and that Taffy was first runner-up. Then she whirled around and stomped off down the hall.

"Jana, are you crazy?" shrieked Beth when we got outside the building. "You said that in front of Mr. Neal."

"So what?" I said. "He doesn't know what it means."

"But he's been to college," Beth insisted. "He probably knows Greek letters."

"Okay, okay. But how could he possibly know that *l* and *r* stand for 'little raisins'?" I asked, trying to sound more confident than I felt.

All the way home I kept wondering if it was possible that Beth was right. I had never felt so stupid in my whole life. I just had to make a good impression on Mr. Neal, especially after the way I'd goofed by not knowing when to stand up and say my name. I had to make him see me for what I really am. What would he think if he figured out what Lambda Rho meant? I'd be so embarrassed that I'd die.

# 4

I nearly worried myself weird for the next few days, but if Mr. Neal understood what Lambda Rho meant, he didn't give himself away. He did something almost as bad, though. He told us to write a five-hundred-word essay entitled "How I Spent My Summer Vacation." The last thing in the world that I wanted to tell anyone about was how I spent my summer vacation.

Sally Schmidt could probably write five hundred pages about her trip to Europe. Taffy Sinclair's parents had a summer cottage on Cape Cod, and Melanie Edwards had gone to Mexico. Even drippy old Clarence Marshall could tell about how he broke his arm. But I couldn't tell anybody about my summer, especially Mr. Neal.

It wasn't what I had done that had made my summer vacation so terrible. It was what I hadn't done. I hadn't gone out west on a two-week vacation with my father, and what was worse, I couldn't figure out why.

I had been on top of the world when I got that letter asking me to go. I hadn't seen him since he and my mother were divorced. I couldn't even remember him. I must have read that letter five thousand times before Mom finally said yes. Then she wrote him giving permission for me to go, and I waited.

I was sure he'd answer soon. I had to know when he was coming for me. After a while, when he didn't write, Mom said that he probably hadn't found out yet when he could take his vacation. I told her that I thought she was right, but deep down I had an awful feeling. All I could think of was that he had asked me to go with him. That was a promise, in a way.

I stationed myself at the mailbox at eleven fifteen every morning. That's the time our mailman usually comes. In fact, I was there so much that I could probably have called my essay, "I Spent My Summer Vacation at the Mailbox."

Around the middle of June Mom said that I should write to him myself and ask him when he was planning to come and explain to him that I needed to know so that I could get ready. She was right, but it took me a whole week just to get out my stationery. I kept giving him one more day. I didn't want to rush him. That would have been embarrassing.

One of the toughest parts of writing to him was figuring out how to start the letter. I tried "Dear Father," "Dear Daddy," and "Dear Dad," but nothing felt right. Those are really personal names to call somebody, especially somebody you can't even remember, A person can't just go around calling people "Father" without the word sticking in her throat unless, of course, she's Catholic, but that's different.

I used to call him "Daddy Bill" in my letters, and that made him seem more like an uncle. I guess I could call just about anybody "Uncle." That's not so personal. But "Daddy Bill" was too babyish for a fifth grader who had been invited on a two-week vacation out west.

He had signed his letter to me "Your Father." I sure couldn't start mine "Dear Your Father." I finally decided to skip that part until later. I could always add it just before I licked the envelope.

The message part of the letter wasn't much easier to write. I would have liked to have skipped it, too. I even thought about sending him a little piece of paper with just my name on it to sort of remind him that I was alive. I thought about it for two whole days. But I knew it wouldn't be the right thing to do. He'd think I was some kind of nut.

What I really wanted to ask him was to explain to me about the divorce. It just didn't make any sense.

Take Mom, for instance. Nobody could be any greater. Even though she works all day and has lots to do when she comes home at night, she's always glad for me to have my friends in. She feeds them and talks to them. And she hardly ever complains about anything except my room. She's really super.

Then there's my father. Mom is always telling me what a wonderful person he is. She says that he's kind and gentle and that he's always the life of the party.

So, like I said, it just didn't make any sense for

two people like that to get divorced. That's why I decided that it must have been somebody else's fault. The worst part about that is that I was the only other person around at the time. That had to be why he hardly ever wrote me letters. He hated me for breaking up him and Mom.

That's a pretty terrible thing to find out about yourself. When I thought about it, which I mostly did after I went to bed at night, my stomach got floppy and my ears got hot. Once I thought I was going to throw up, but I didn't. I just lay there in the dark asking myself over and over again what on earth I could have done. It must have been pretty grim.

I tried to think of what a baby could do. Mom said I cried a lot. In fact, I guess I cried pretty much all the time for a while. But you couldn't hate a baby just because it cried.

No, it must have been something else. Maybe it was something that happened when I was three, since that was how old I was when they got divorced. I couldn't remember being three. I racked my brain trying to think if I'd ever been told anything about myself when I was three that would give me a clue. All I knew was that I'd had pneumonia. You sure couldn't turn against a little kid for getting sick.

I had asked Mom about the divorce lots of time, and she always said that when I was older she would explain. Well, I get older every day, and I understand all kinds of things that I didn't used to understand, but she still hasn't explained it.

My father was my only hope, but I didn't have the nerve to write that kind of letter. Besides, maybe he had forgiven me, and that was why he had

invited me on a two-week vacation out west. What I
finally wrote was just three sentences.

> I hope I'll be hearing from you soon. I
> need to know when you're coming to take
> me out west so that I can get my things
> packed. I can't wait to go.
> Love,
> Jana

Just as I dropped it into the mailbox I remembered the "Dear" part. I had forgotten to go back
and put that on. I almost died.

Anyway, nothing else happened all summer. I
never did hear from my father. I never did go on a
two-week vacation out west. And I never did figure
out what I had done to cause my parents to get a
divorce. It was an awful summer. How could I put
that into an essay for Mr. Neal? I hadn't even been
able to talk about it to my friends.

Then I got this great idea. Mr. Neal didn't know
how I spent my summer vacation. For all he knew, I
might have really gone out west. I went to the library and checked out a lot of books. I read up on all
kinds of places like the Grand Canyon and Pike's
Peak and the Painted Desert. Then I remembered
this other book I had read. It was all about a girl who
spent a summer on a ranch. She had a lot of exciting
adventures like getting lost on a pack trip in the
mountains and getting thrown by her horse and
breaking her leg while she was all alone and finally
getting rescued in the middle of a terrible storm just
minutes before a mud slide covered up the spot
where she had been. The more I thought about it,
the more excited I got. I'd write about it as if it had

happened to me. It would be the greatest essay in the whole fifth grade.

I really slaved over that essay. I never worked so hard on anything in my whole life. I changed a few things in the story, though. For instance, I said that I just sprained my ankle when I fell off the horse since broken bones take a long time to heal and Mr. Neal might wonder where my cast was or why I didn't limp or something.

The essay was due on Friday. I wanted to go straight home after school on Thursday and get it finished, but I had to go to Melanie Edwards' house for a Lambda Rho meeting.

I called the meeting to order, and Christie, who is treasurer, reported that we had seventeen cents in our treasury left over from last year. Then she collected ten cents dues from everybody, bringing the total up to sixty-seven cents.

"That's sure a long way from nineteen ninety-five," said Katie, shaking her head.

"Has anybody thought up a good money-making scheme?" I asked hopefully.

Nobody had, so Beth suggested that we keep thinking about it until the next meeting. Then I asked for the reports on Taffy Sinclair.

"I have one," said Melanie. She stood up and opened her Against Taffy Sinclair Club notebook. "September fifteen, one-oh-seven P.M. Math class. Taffy Sinclair goes to Mr. Neal's desk and asks for help on a problem. Bats eyes and smiles sickeningly. Mr. Neal smiles."

My heart jumped into my throat. Math! I remembered how I had dreamed of going to him with my math problems, and now Taffy Sinclair was beating me at my own game. I couldn't let her get away with a thing like that. I'd think of some fantastic way to raise that nineteen ninety-five. Then I'd show her.

There weren't any other reports on Taffy, so Beth asked if she could have the floor. "Even if we had the nineteen ninety-five right now, it would take a while to order the Milo Venus Bust Developer and get it through the mail," she said. "In the meantime, we can't just sit around doing nothing and let Taffy Sinclair get farther and farther ahead of us."

There were nods and murmurs of agreement and Beth got that old mysterious look on her face again.

"I've got another plan," she whispered gleefully. Then she reached into her book bag and pulled out a long, blue measuring tape like the one Mom keeps in her sewing basket.

"This . . ." Beth said, holding up the measuring tape, "and this . . ." she waved her Against Taffy Sinclair Club notebook in the other hand, ". . . is going to take the place of our Milo Venus Bust Developer until it arrives."

We must all have had puzzled looks on our faces because she began talking fast.

"First, we'll each make a chart on the back page of our Against Taffy Sinclair Club notebooks. Then we'll measure our chests and record the measurement under today's date. After that, we'll start doing some special chest-developing exercises that I happen to know about. Every day we'll do our exercises and once a week we'll measure. That way we can keep track of our progress. Okay, who wants to measure first?"

I looked down at the floor so that no one would

think that I was volunteering. I'm about the size of your standard third grader, which isn't so bad if you're in the third grade, or even the fourth. But if you're in the fifth, it's dismal, and I certainly didn't want anybody to know my measurements.

Nobody else volunteered, either.

"Well, you don't have to do it in front of everybody," Beth finally said with disgust. "Go into the bathroom. You go first, Jana, since you're the president."

Grudgingly I took the tape measure and went into the bathroom. I closed the door and punched the lock in the doorknob, even though I knew that nobody would try to barge in. I slipped the tape around my chest, took a deep breath and looked. I couldn't believe my eyes. I measured thirty-four inches!

I knew it was too good to be true. The tape was twisted. I straightened it out and looked again. I was a lousy twenty-six.

After everybody had measured and recorded their measurements in their notebooks, Beth demonstrated the exercises. First, she showed us how to straighten out the fingers on each hand and press the tips together as hard as we could. One-two-three-four. Rest. One-two-three-four. Rest. Then we clasped our hands together and pulled as if we were trying to break a tug of war. One-two-three-four. Rest. One-two-three-four. Rest. Over and over again we pushed and pulled. Those exercises sure used the right muscles—I could tell that much—but it was hard to believe that they would do much good.

Anyway, that night after I had finished my essay and had it ready to turn in, I did each exercise an extra twenty times. I measured again. Still twenty-six. Well, it was a little too soon to get results. Finally I slipped into bed, and until I fell asleep, I tried as hard as I could to think of some way to raise $19.95.

# 5

_____

The idea came to me the next day in the school lunchroom. It was so great and so simple that I don't know why none of us had thought of it before.

I had just finished a jelly and cream-cheese sandwich, a hard-boiled egg, a bag of potato chips, a Coke, and an apple, and I was still a little bit hungry. Melanie was sitting across the table from me stuffing a gorgeous brownie into her mouth. It looked so delicious I thought I'd die. Finally I got up and went to the candy machine, but everything there was twenty cents and I only had fifteen.

Then I got this great idea. We could sell brownies in the lunchroom! It would be a cinch. We could get Melanie's mother's recipe. Then we could pool our allowances to buy the stuff we needed. If we went to my apartment right after school, we could get the brownies made before Mom got home from work. That way none of our parents would know about it and ask a lot of embarrassing questions about what we were going to buy with the money we earned. We could each take home some of the brownies so that they would be easier to hide. Then the next day we could bring them to school and sell them. How could anything be simpler?

"I'll bet every kid in school will buy one," said Beth when I'd finished explaining my plan. "We'll get rich!"

Everybody liked my idea except Katie. She said that it was another example of role stereotyping and that we should do something with less social stigma attached, like mowing lawns or washing cars. We decided to make brownies anyway, but since it was Friday and most of us get our allowances on Saturday, we decided to wait until after school Monday to go to the grocery store. That would give Melanie all weekend to sneak her mother's recipe. Tuesday we would make the brownies, and Wednesday would be the big day.

Saturday afternoon the phone rang. It was Melanie. She sounded as if she were crying.

"Mom is making brownies," she said between sniffs. "And guess what?"

I couldn't.

"She doesn't use a recipe! I asked her why and she said that she makes them so often that she knows how much of everything to use. What are we going to do?"

My heart sank into my shoes. We couldn't make brownies without a recipe, but Melanie was crying again so I tried to reassure her.

"Don't worry, Melanie," I said. "We'll think of something."

I hung up the phone and sauntered into the

31

kitchen. Mom was there humming to herself while she got a roast ready for the oven. Mom never makes brownies. She doesn't have time since she works every day. Not that she doesn't do special things for me. She does. It's just that making brownies isn't one of them. I started to leave. Then I noticed the shelf of cookbooks over the stove. Why hadn't I thought of that before! Surely there would be a brownie recipe in one of them.

I got a drink of water, and looked at the cookbooks out of the corner of my eye. Reading cookbooks was something I never did. Mom would get suspicious and start asking a lot of questions if I just grabbed one and started thumbing through it. I got another drink of water while I thought about the situation. There wasn't much I could do except wait until Mom wasn't around.

She was around all weekend. I couldn't remember when she had been around so much. Worst of all, it seemed that she was always in the kitchen. She even cleaned out the cupboards, which she hardly ever does. I almost got the feeling that she knew I was up to something.

By Sunday night I was feeling desperate. I couldn't let everybody down. After all, I was the president of the club and selling brownies had been my idea. But I couldn't think of any way to get that cookbook without Mom seeing me. I tried to sit down and watch television with her, but I was so antsy that I could just barely sit there.

Then Pink came over. Pink is short for Wallace Pinkerton, and he and Mom go out together once in a while. They both work at the newspaper. Mom is the Classified Advertising manager and Pink is one of the printers. He's tall and blond and very nice looking. I like him a lot, but there's just one problem with Pink. He has breath that would stop a tidal wave. Mom once said that their relationship was purely platonic, and after one whiff of his breath, I had to believe her. Either that or else her olfactory nerves have konked out.

Anyway, when Pink came in, it gave me a perfect excuse to go to my room. I said a quick hello and ducked out before he had a chance to breathe on me. Once I got into the privacy of my own room I began to pace up and down like mad. I had to think of something—and fast.

Every so often I'd open my bedroom door a crack to see what Mom and Pink were doing. They were always doing the same thing, just sitting right there in plain sight of the cookbooks watching a horror movie on television. If only Pink would do something to distract her, I thought, like kiss her or something. Maybe then I could tear into the kitchen and grab a cookbook and she would never know it. Then I remembered his breath and I knew that that was out.

Once, while I was pacing, a lady in the movie let out a blood-curdling scream, and I nearly jumped out of my skin. How could I ever get an inspiration with a thing like that going on? I couldn't. Finally I wound my alarm clock, did my exercises, recorded my measurements, and went to bed in defeat.

Then I got this great idea. My alarm was set for seven o'clock in the morning. I changed it to midnight. Mom would be asleep by then. I would get up, slip into the kitchen, and get one of her cookbooks. I would bring it to my room, copy a brownie recipe, and then sneak the cookbook back into the kitchen without Mom ever knowing it.

Little shivers raced up and down my back as I reset my alarm clock. This was going to be exciting. I had only been up until midnight a couple of times in my whole life. It would be pitch dark in the apartment, but I wasn't going to be afraid.

I was too excited to go to sleep, so I lay there in the darkness listening for Pink to go home. I thought that he would never leave. Didn't he know that Mom had to get up and go to work the next day? I was beginning to think that he would stay all night when I finally heard him go. I looked at my clock. It was ten forty-five. Just one hour and fifteen minutes to zero.

After that, I just couldn't lie still. I felt as if I were hovering about half an inch above the bed. I must have finally dozed off, because when the alarm sounded I nearly went through the ceiling. It was never that loud in the morning. What if Mom had heard it? After I shut it off, I lay there for a long time listening, but I didn't hear anything. Mom must have slept right through it.

The first thing I did after I got up was fall down. I tripped over my sneakers which, as usual, I had left in the middle of the floor. When I fell it sounded as though the building were caving in so I lay there for a while listening for Mom. I opened my eyes wide in the dark and swept a hand across the floor feeling for anything else that I might have pitched around. I didn't find anything so I whispered "Neatness counts" five times under my breath, got up again, and tiptoed toward the door.

I felt like a cat burglar sneaking across the living room and into the kitchen. It gave me a creepy feeling, but at the same time, it was sort of fun. My eyes were getting used to the darkness, so I was able to walk like a normal person instead of like a sleepwalker with my arms stuck out in front. Just as I pulled a cookbook off the shelf and started for my room, I heard this thunk. Mom was awake!

I ducked behind a chair and listened. I could hear traffic in the street and my own heart beating but no more thunks. Probably she had just rolled over in her sleep and kicked the wall or something. When I got back to my room I closed the door without a sound and turned on my desk light. I looked at the cookbook in my hand. *The Pleasures of Chinese Cooking.* I couldn't believe it. I knew there wouldn't be any brownie recipe in a Chinese cookbook, but I looked anyway. I was right. There was nothing to do but get another book.

When I turned off my light the place looked darker than ever. I inched along like a snail, praying that I hadn't left any of my junk around on the living room floor. As I slipped into the kitchen, I knew what I would have to do. I would have to turn on the light just long enough to find an American cookbook, one that would have a brownie recipe in it. Otherwise, I could spend the whole night running back and forth in the dark with cookbooks.

I hesitated for a minute. Turning on the light was going to be dangerous, but it was the only thing to do.

I took a deep breath and flipped the switch. The light was so bright that I had to squint my eyes and look out through my lashes. The third book from the left was *the* book. I was absolutely certain of it. It was the *Better Homes and Gardens New*

*Cookbook.* I slipped it under my arm, turned the light off, and felt my way back to my room.

I was right about the *Better Homes and Gardens New Cookbook.* It had three brownie recipes in it, Jiffy, Nutty, and Remarkable. I wanted to pick Remarkable because it sounded the best, but I settled on Jiffy because it was the easiest.

After I had copied the recipe and put the cookbook back on the shelf, I looked at my clock. It was twelve thirty-six A.M. I wasn't a bit sleepy, so I reset my alarm and did my bust-developing exercises another twenty times before I got into bed.

I didn't hear my alarm, and Mom had to shake me to wake me up. I couldn't believe that it was morning. I felt as if I'd been up all night. Sitting at my school desk was really grim. Even the sight of gorgeous Mr. Neal couldn't keep my eyelids open. I thought about getting a drink and splashing some of the water on my face. But he'd think I had to go to the bathroom if I raised my hand to leave the room. So, instead, I crossed my arms and sat there pinching my sides until I wasn't feeling so sleepy anymore.

At noon I showed everybody the recipe and Christie figured that by quadrupling the ingredients and charging fifteen cents apiece for the brownies we would make $21.05. That would be more than enough to pay for the bust developer.

It was too good to be true. We were so delirious that the lunchroom monitor had to tell us to be quiet. We couldn't have cared less. Just two more days and the Milo Venus Bust Developer would be ours.

# 6

I have this theory about lying. If you make up a big-enough lie, people are going to believe it. What I mean is that anybody can make up a little lie. That's no big deal. But most people swallow a whopper because they don't think anyone has the brains to make it up, much less the nerve to tell it. Take my essay, for instance. Now that was a whopper. I have never been west of Morristown, New Jersey, where my grandmother lives, and the closest thing to horseback riding that I've ever done is the pony ride at the Danbury Fair.

Mr. Neal believed my essay. He believed it so much that he gave me an A minus. The minus was for misspelling "terrain." I spelled it "terrane." He told the class how good my essay was. He said it was the best essay in the whole fifth grade.

I sure was sorry that it was so good. I would have given anything if it had been lousy. Then he would have handed it back to me the way he did all the others, and I could have burned it or torn it up into little tiny pieces and swallowed it so that nobody could read it. Instead, he announced to the class that he had given my essay to Mrs. Lockwood, the faculty adviser for the school newspaper, and that it was going to be printed on the front page for the whole school to read.

I thought I'd die. All of my friends knew that I hadn't spent my summer vacation out west. Probably even Taffy Sinclair knew the truth. She might tell Mr. Neal! And what made it even worse, the paper would come out on Wednesday, the day we were going to sell brownies.

After school Beth, Christie, Melanie, Katie, and I met on the playground to pool our money for the ingredients for the brownies. Me and my great ideas. The last thing I wanted was to sell brownies on the same day the whole school found out that I was a liar. I could just picture myself slinking around the lunchroom like some kind of criminal.

"Why don't we wait until next week?" I said, trying to sound lighthearted. "This week everybody will be too busy reading the paper to care about eating brownies."

"Are you kidding?" shrieked Melanie. "Most kids would stop to eat brownies if the school was on fire."

"Well, maybe it's against the law to sell food without a license or something," I offered.

"Naw," said Katie, making a face. "Remember last year when our Girl Scout troop had a bake sale? We didn't need a license then. Why should we need one now?"

I knew that I was defeated, so I dug down into

the pocket of my jeans and pulled out a crumpled dollar bill.

"Here," I said, and I handed it to Christie, who was laboriously marking down every contribution in her notebook.

"That does it," she announced triumphantly. "Fellow members of Lambda Rho, our mission is almost accomplished."

Everybody started cheering and giggling and jumping around. I tried to join in, but my heart just wasn't in it. Everybody kept giving me funny looks. I knew they were wondering why I was so quiet. As far as they were concerned my life was just about perfect. My essay was going to be printed on the front page of the school newspaper; we were going to make a lot of money selling brownies; and the Milo Venus Bust Developer was almost ours. Fame, fortune, and a figure. They probably thought I should be dancing in the streets.

I really wanted to talk to them about my problem, but it was too embarrassing to admit even to my four best friends. I made up an excuse about having an earache and said I thought I'd go on home. They didn't need me anyway. Katie and Christie had volunteered to do the grocery shopping.

Suddenly it was Tuesday. I kept telling myself that at least it wasn't Wednesday, but that wasn't much consolation. The school day went pretty well except for math class. Mr. Neal called on me three times, and I didn't know the answer even once. That was the first time all year that I'd been called on and hadn't known the answer.

After school everybody raced to my apartment to make the brownies. Beth was in command and she whipped out her copy of *Redbook* as soon as we got there. She turned to the advertisement for the Milo Venus Bust Developer and propped the magazine up on the counter. "For inspiration!" she said. "Okay, where's the recipe and the ingredients and the pots and pans? Let's get started."

"Yuk!" said Katie, who was rummaging around in her book bag. "I accidentally put my social-studies book on top of the cream cheese and it got all smushed. I think we can still use it, though." Using two fingers, she pulled a squashed package of cream cheese out of the book bag and dropped it on the counter. Then she brought out a sack of sugar, a sack of flour, a package of walnuts, and a bar of unsweetened chocolate squares. "I hope you have vanilla, Jana. We didn't buy any."

I nodded and tried to swallow away the lump that was forming in my throat. We were really going to make the brownies. And tomorrow was really going to get here. And my essay was really going to be on the front page of the school paper for everybody to read. And there wasn't a single thing that I could do about it.

I got out all the stuff they needed and stood back in the corner. I didn't want to help. I stood there listening to Beth read the recipe out loud. She could have won an Oscar for the way she read it. I never heard anyone read a recipe like that. It sounded like something out of Shakespeare.

Everybody was measuring and stirring and giggling. I just stood there.

"Quickly stir in the melted chocolate," said Beth.

Suddenly I couldn't stand it any longer. I took a deep breath and yelled as loudly as I could, "My essay that's going to be on the front page of the school paper tomorrow is a big, fat *lie!*"

There was instant silence. The measuring, stirring, and giggling all stopped. From the looks on their faces you would have thought that I had just announced that I had a rare, fatal blood disease or something. A *contagious*, rare, fatal blood disease.

"A lie?" whispered Beth. "What are you going to do?"

They all looked so silly standing there with their mouths hanging open, except for Melanie, who was licking chocolate off a spoon and staring at me with doleful eyes, that I suddenly felt calm. "I'm going to blow up the school," I said. "What else can I do?"

Christie gave a disgusted look. "What are you really going to do?"

I shrugged and sat down on a kitchen chair.

"What if Mr. Neal finds out that it's lie?"

"Could you get expelled for a thing like that?"

"I'm sure glad that I'm not you."

"We've got to go ahead and sell the brownies since we've already started making them."

"Thanks a lot for cheering me up," I said. Looking embarrassed, all four of them turned around and quietly finished the brownies.

Why is it that when you're looking forward to something, time takes forever to pass, but when it's something you don't want to happen, a whole day can go by in about half a minute? Before I knew it, it was time to go to bed. I lay there as long as I could, humming, reciting my multiplication tables, doing anything I could think of to keep myself awake because I knew that as soon as I closed my eyes it would be morning again. Doomsday.

And sure enough, it was. I faced the breakfast table the way a condemned prisoner faces his last meal, and I had the awful feeling that the two eggs on my plate were staring at me. Even *they* probably knew that I hadn't spent my summer vacation out west.

I had given up trying to figure out what to do. What I really wanted to do was to run away, but there was no place to go. I didn't have any money so I couldn't check into a hotel. My grandmother in Morristown, New Jersey, is the world's greatest worrier, so I couldn't go there. She'd be sure to turn me in.

I even thought of hitchhiking to Poughkeepsie, where my father lives. That was the plan I liked best, but I couldn't make up my mind whether to barge right in on him or to shadow him for a few days and peek in his windows at him until I knew him a little better.

When I was a lot younger I used to make up stories about what he was like. You see, when you don't really know someone, you can do a thing like that. You can make the person into anything you want him to be. Mostly I made my father into a spy who couldn't reveal his true identity even to Mom and me because he was constantly in mortal danger and didn't want us to be in danger, too. That was why he couldn't write much or even come to see me. The story always had a happy ending, though. He would retire from being a spy and come to live with us and tell us all about his adventures and show us his souvenirs and things.

But deep down I always knew it wasn't really true, just the way, deep down, I knew I wasn't going to run away. Not even to Poughkeepsie.

42

All through breakfast Mom kept chirping away about what a beautiful morning it was and how I'd better hurry so that I'd have time to enjoy my walk to school, but I waited as long as I could to leave. I stuffed my books into my book bag and almost forgot my share of the brownies, which I had stashed under my bed.

All the way to school I kept thinking about what it would be like when Mrs. Lockwood delivered the school newspaper to our room and everybody read my essay. Mrs. Lockwood is sort of flighty and goes off on tangents a lot, so we never know exactly what time she'll bring the papers around. Anyway, you can always tell when she's coming before she gets there. She wears these clicky shoes and she walks fast, sort of skipping, so that it sounds as though she's tap-dancing up the hall. You can hear her a mile away.

When I got to school I ducked into the girl's bathroom, partly because I didn't want to face anyone, not even my friends, and partly because I felt as if I were going to throw up. I went into one of the stalls and leaned against the door. It was made of metal and felt cool through my blouse.

Pretty soon the first bell rang. I knew that if I was going to do anything, like run away, I only had five more minutes. After that, it would be too late.

I closed my eyes, and a picture of Taffy Sinclair bobbed into my mind. She was holding the school newspaper and laughing like crazy. She almost never smiles big or laughs like that because she has one crooked bicuspid, which she doesn't like people to see. But there she was, laughing away, crooked bicuspid and all.

I nearly shot over the top of the stall when the

final bell rang. I knew I was jumpy, but that had really been a fast five minutes. My doom was sealed now, I would have to go to my room.

Out in the hall everybody was tearing around and banging lockers and racing for their classes. Everybody but me. It would have taken a calendar to time me. The hall was quiet by the time I finally got to the fifth-grade room, and Mr. Neal was already taking the roll.

I sort of melted down into my seat, trying not to be any more noticeable than I had to be. Mr. Neal kept on taking the roll. Naturally everybody in the whole fifth grade was present.

Melanie passed me a note asking if I'd remembered to bring my share of the brownies. The thought of brownies made me gag, but I nodded to her that I had. All my friends gave me sympathetic looks. I knew they felt sorry for me, but it didn't help one bit.

The first period of the day is always history. Usually I'm glad it's first because it's so dull and boring and I like to get it over with for the day, but today I almost couldn't stand it. We were studying the Battle of Fredricksburg in the Civil War. I sat there wishing that I had been in the Civil War, even the Battle of Fredricksburg, because if I had I'd be dead by now and wouldn't have to worry about anybody reading my essay.

History period went on and on forever. I didn't think it would ever end. Once I thought I heard Mrs. Lockwood's clicky shoes in the hall, but it must have been something else. Finally it was ten o'clock, time to put away the history books.

The next period was reading. Mr. Neal announced that today we would have free reading and a cheer went up from the class. Everybody likes free reading because you can write notes and stuff if you're careful while you pretend you're really absorbed in a book.

I went back to the bookshelves in the reading center and took *Cowslip* off the shelf. I picked *Cowslip* because I had already read it three times and practically knew it by heart. That way if Mr. Neal asked questions about what we had read, which he does sometimes, I would be sure to know the answers.

I slouched down into my seat and propped the book up in front of me so that Mr. Neal couldn't see my face. That way I wouldn't have to make my eyes go back and forth as if I were really reading. All I had to do was remember to turn the page once in a while.

I closed my eyes and listened as hard as I could for Mrs. Lockwood's clicky shoes. I believe that a person can hear better with her eyes closed because she isn't distracted by all the things she sees. I explained this theory to my fourth-grade teacher once when she caught me with my eyes closed and thought I was sleeping, but I wasn't able to convince her. I've been careful about practicing my theory ever since, and so I opened one eye every few minutes to make sure Mr. Neal wasn't standing over my desk looking at me or something. I listened as hard as I could for the whole hour. I heard kids' feet scraping back and forth under their desks. I heard kids sharpening their pencils. I heard Beth Barry blowing her nose. I even heard pages being turned. But I didn't hear Mrs. Lockwood's clicky shoes.

On Mondays, Wednesdays, and Fridays we go

45

to the music room at eleven. Our music teacher is Miss Crocker, only we're suppose to call her Ms. Crocker. She must weigh three hundred pounds, and when she plays a fast song on the piano the fat on the underside of her arms flops like crazy. It's really something to see. She sits on the piano bench with her back to the class playing and singing her head off. Sometimes she gets so carried away that she doesn't know the kids are fooling around instead of singing with her. Once a boy named Joey Roberts slipped out of the music room and sneaked all the way to a grocery store across the street from the school. He bought a big bag of cheese popcorn, which he brought back and shared with the whole class. Ms. Crocker didn't see a thing. She just kept right on playing and singing "When The Saints Go Marching In." You'd have thought she would at least have smelled the popcorn.

The worst thing about being in the music room is that with all that racket it's almost impossible to hear anything going on in the hall. I tried to get a seat near the door so that I could hear better, but a bunch of boys beat me out. They always sit by the door since Music is the last period before lunch and they like to go tearing out when the bell rings so that they can be first in line at the cafeteria. I found a seat as close to the door as I could and pretended not to notice that my friends had saved me a place near the front and were waving like mad for me to come up there.

As long as things were quiet, I was pretty calm. But as soon as Ms. Crocker started playing "This Old Man" I panicked. Mrs. Lockwood could burst in on us any minute and I wouldn't be prepared.

By the fourth chorus I couldn't stand it any

longer, and I got up and went to the door. I put my ear against it but all I could hear was the music, so I opened it a crack. Thank goodness the hall was empty. Mrs. Lockwood wasn't clicking yet. I slipped back into my seat just as the song was over and Ms. Crocker turned around. So far, my luck was holding out.

# 7

When the lunch bell rang everybody piled into the cafeteria. The hot-lunch kids were grabbing trays and lining up by the steam tables. Mom is always raving that I should have a hot lunch instead of taking a cream-cheese-and-jelly-sandwich every day. She wouldn't say that if she had ever tasted the cafeteria food. Today, for instance, they were serving Alpo. That's what we kids call the corned-beef hash. Christie Winchell has a dog, and she tasted Alpo once. She says it tastes better than the corned-beef hash the school serves.

Anyway, since I got out of the music room ahead of my friends, I got to the cafeteria first, too, and got us a super table in the corner by a window. I felt pretty relieved as I sat down. At least Mrs. Lockwood hadn't delivered the newspapers before it was time to sell the brownies. I was really thankful for that.

While I was watching for my friends, Taffy

Sinclair came into the cafeteria and got into the Alpo line. Mona Vaughn was tagging along behind her. Finally Christie, Melanie, and Beth came in and plopped their lunch sacks down on the table.

"Where's Katie?" I asked.

"She had to go back to Mr. Neal's room," said Melanie. "I guess she must have forgotten something."

"Katie forgot something?" I said. "You've got to be kidding."

A minute later Katie stepped inside the cafeteria door. She was really loaded down. Besides her lunch, she had her book bag and a huge piece of cardboard with brown grocery sacks Scotch-taped all over one side. She put everything down on the table nearest the door and started looking around for the rest of us. As soon as she saw us she started frowning and motioning like crazy for us to go to where she was.

We all frowned and shook our heads and waved for her to come where we were. The table nearest the door is the worst one in the whole cafeteria and always the last one anyone sits at. The reason is that there is a large trash can right next to it where kids throw away their lunch sacks, milk cartons, and half-eaten sandwiches as they leave. That wouldn't be so bad except that lots of kids think that they're Wilt the Stilt and pitch their stuff from the middle of the room. Only about half of it hits the trash can, and most of the time at least some of it lands on that table. A person would have to be crazy to *want* to sit there.

When she saw that we weren't going to budge, she left her stuff on the table and came storming over to us.

"What are you doing in this corner?" she de-

manded. "We've got to be by the door if we are
going to sell any brownies. We have to display our
merchandise where everyone can see it, and every
single person has to pass that table to get out of this
cafeteria."

There was no arguing with Katie. Besides we
all knew she was right. With a large groan we
gathered up our sandwiches, sacks, and junk and
followed her to the table by the door. You would
have thought that she was leading an army into battle, and she started giving orders before any of us
could sit down.

"Don't anybody take a bite," she said. "Some
kids have already finished eating. We've got to get
our merchandise out where they can see it, and
we've got to do it in a hurry."

Swell, I thought. I was beginning to feel faint
with hunger and my stomach sounded like a thun-
derstorm, but I got out my share of the "merchandise" and shoved it across the table toward Katie.

Everybody else did the same thing, but Katie
was too busy to pay much attention. She was ripping
the grocery sacks off the big piece of cardboard. It
turned out to be a sign. In big red letters she had
written, "Homemade Brownies for Sale—15¢." Underneath that was a big brown glob, which I guess
was supposed to look like a brownie. Even if the
artwork wasn't so hot, I had to admit that having a
sign was a pretty smart thing.

Katie propped the sign up against the table and
then hit us with another bombshell. "Did everybody bring some change?"

"Change?" asked Beth.

"Hey, that's a good idea," said Melanie.

"Of course it's a good idea," said Katie in a really disgusted voice. She opened her book bag and

pulled out an empty egg carton and a change purse and began separating pennies, nickels, and dimes into different sections of the carton. "I brought fifty-eight cents out of my bank to help us get started."

The rest of us looked at each other sheepishly. I could just picture Katie Shannon as the president of her own company someday. She'll probably run the whole thing singlehandedly. Of course her company won't make brownies. She'll probably own a refinery and make motor oil or something. There was no doubt about it, though, Katie was the real brains in our club. I was just about to tell her so when she started in again.

"If women are going to take their rightful place in society, they're going to have to be more organized and take a more businesslike approach. Women are going to have to learn—"

Just then Clarence Marshall spotted our sign and started to shout. "Hey, look, everybody! Brownies! They're selling brownies!"

You would have thought that he had announced free samples from the United States Mint. Suddenly we were swamped with kids. They were swarming around us and dropping money onto the table and grabbing brownies as fast as they could. One sixth-grade boy even tried to buy my cream-cheese-and-jelly sandwich. I wouldn't have sold it to him for five dollars. I was practically starved.

Mona Vaughn bought two brownies. Out of the corner of my eye I could see her giving one of them to Taffy Sinclair. Taffy looked at it for a minute as if she thought it might be poison, but then she took a bite. I couldn't help but grin. Taffy would die if she knew what that money was going for.

We were out of brownies in just about half a

minute, or at least it seemed that fast. We could have sold twice as many if we'd had them. Lots of kids were really mad that they didn't get one. We didn't care. From the looks of that egg carton we had plenty of money for the Milo Venus Bust Developer. We were so happy that we started giggling and hopping around and making so much racket that the lunchroom monitor had to ask us to settle down. We cleaned up the crumbs and pitched the sign into the trash can and finally sat down to eat.

Just as I took a big, delicious bite of my cream-cheese-and-jelly sandwich, I heard Katie yelp. A big fat apple core was lying right on top of her baloney sandwich. I winced. Somebody had missed the trash can again. I ducked my head. I couldn't look at her. I knew I'd have that "I told you so" look on my face if I did. I sneaked a look at Melanie, Beth, and Christie. They weren't looking at her either.

We just barely had finished eating when the bell rang. My heart nearly stopped. I had been having such a good time selling brownies that I had forgotten all about my essay and the school newspaper. Now it was time for math class, time to start listening for Mrs. Lockwood's clicky shoes again. Maybe she wouldn't get around to passing out the papers until late in the afternoon, just before it was time to go home, and the kids wouldn't have time to read them before they left school. It was too good to hope for, but I hoped it anyway. I hoped it all the way back to the fifth-grade room.

Just as I was getting interested in the math lesson, which was the most relaxed I'd been in class all day, I heard them. I listened hard to be sure. It was them, all right. Mrs. Lockwood's clicky shoes. She was still a long way away, down at the other end of the hall. She was coming, though. There was no doubt about it. Zero hour was almost here.

Suddenly I started going numb. My arms and legs felt as though they were floating off in space. I touched my nose. At least I still had feeling there. The clicking stopped. She had probably gone into another classroom. Maybe she would stay in there and talk to the teacher for a while. Maybe the door would get stuck and she wouldn't be able to get out and they would have to call the custodian to take the door off the hinges. You could never find him when you needed him, so that could take all day.

No such luck. She was clicking again. Was I going crazy? She was double-clicking this time! No, she wasn't. It was Mr. Neal writing a problem on the blackboard. She was in another classroom. She hardly stayed there long enough to hand the papers to the teacher. She must have pitched them in the door and run. The clicking was getting louder. It didn't sound so much like tap-dancing today. It sounded more like machine-gun fire.

I cleared my throat and tried to concentrate on the problem on the board. Mr. Neal was explaining it, but his voice sounded far away, and I couldn't understand the words.

Then the door opened, and Mrs. Lockwood came bouncing in. She had an armload of papers, and she gave me a big grin when she passed by. She sort of tipped the papers and pointed to my name right there on the front page.

My stomach began doing flip-flops, and I had a puckery feeling in the back of my mouth. I started to raise my hand to ask to leave the room. I didn't even care if Mr. Neal thought I had to go to the bathroom. My lunch was rising toward my throat. I knew I didn't have time to raise my hand, so I just stood up and raced for the door. My lunch was racing, too, and the door was still five miles away. I knew I couldn't make it. That awful taste was in my mouth. I stopped, and then I threw up on my shoes.

# 8

The school nurse let me lie down on a cot while she called Mom at the newspaper to come for me. Then she excused herself, saying that if I'd be all right alone she would take care of some things in another part of the school. I don't think she really had anything else to do. I think she couldn't stand the way my sneakers smelled.

I really felt sort of important lying there in spite of the fact that I had just thrown up in front of Mr. Neal, Mrs. Lockwood, and the whole fifth-grade class. The truth is that I've never broken any records or done much to distinguish myself unless you count my third-grade napkin. Mom says that I'm probably the only kid in the world who carried the same paper napkin in her lunch box for an entire school year and never got so much as a smudge on it. But then nobody but Mom and me ever knew about that.

Still, I guess I was glad to be in the nurse's office because I knew that at that very moment everybody was reading my essay.

All the same, but I couldn't stay there for the rest of my life, and I had started getting antsy when Mom walked in wearing her "worried-mother" look. She felt my forehead and cheeks about every two seconds while she waited for the nurse to get back.

I was feeling perfectly fine by the time we got home, but I didn't let on. Mom might have sent me back to school. Instead, I pretended to feel awful, and I got my pajamas on and went to bed as soon as I could. Mom got out the thermometer and the Pepto Bismol, and I let her go through her hospital routine and then told her that I was sleepy. She said that sleep would do me more good than anything and that she'd go make some Jello. She always feeds me Jello when I'm sick.

The moment my bedroom door closed, I sat up. What in the world was I going to do? Throwing up in school had only made things worse. How had I gotten myself into such an embarrassing situation?

I was sorry that I had asked myself that question. The answer was too terrible to be true. If he hadn't invited me on a two-week vacation out west, none of this would have happened. I wouldn't have written that stupid essay and gotten so nervous that I'd thrown up in front of the whole fifth-grade class.

It was probably his fault that I was flat-chested, too. Probably all the women in his family clear back to prehistoric times had been flat-chested. Mom wasn't flat-chested. Poor Mom. I almost cried, thinking of her out there in the kitchen making Jello for me and taking care of me all by herself. I could

56

sure see now whose fault it was that they got a divorce. I didn't know why she always told me he was
so great. Maybe she didn't want me to know the
awful truth.

I knew that I had to do something. I couldn't
just let my father get away with a thing like that. If I
didn't do something, he'd go on forever thinking
that he had me fooled. But what could I do?

Then I got this great idea. I knew that I was a
pretty good writer. Hadn't I written the best essay
in the whole fifth grade? I'd write him a letter, and
in it I'd tell him about all the humiliation and misery that he had caused. It would be a masterpiece,
even better than my essay. When he read it, he
would feel terrible. Maybe he would even cry. And
he would call me up long distance to tell me how
bad he felt and say that he was going to make it up to
Mom and me.

I tiptoed to my desk and got my stationery and a
pen and then crawled back into bed. I remembered
what a hard time I'd had starting that letter to him
before and how I had sealed it without going back
and putting the "Dear" part in. I knew exactly how I
wanted to start this one. I could already see the
words inside my head, and I began to write as fast as
I could so that I wouldn't forget anything before I
got it all down on paper.

"I can't start this letter 'Dear Father' because
you've never been much of a father to me, and after
all the trouble you've caused, I don't think you're
very dear!"

I went on to tell him how Mom had always said
that he was a super person, but that now I knew the
truth. I told him how disappointed I had been not to
go on a two-week vacation out west after he had

asked me to go and about my essay and about throwing up on my shoes. I wrote on and on until I had three pages. Surely now he would see what he had done.

I sealed the envelope and flopped back onto my pillow. I was exhausted, but there was one more thing that I had to do. I had to talk to Mom. I knew she'd feel better when she understood that I already knew the truth about my father. I lay there and practiced a speech for a while. It sounded pretty good in my head.

She came in later to check on me, but I pretended that I was still asleep. I hadn't finished practicing my speech. I couldn't take a chance on goofing it up.

Finally I got so hungry that I couldn't lie there any longer, and I got up and went into the kitchen to see if the Jello was set. It wasn't. Mom said I could have some tea and crackers because they were good for an upset stomach, too.

Tea and crackers were just about the last thing I wanted. I had seen some leftover spaghetti when I opened the refrigerator to check the Jello. I could have gobbled that spaghetti down in just about half a second, even cold, but I knew that I had to play the role.

Mom started making the tea, taking care of me again, and I decided that the time had come. "Mom," I said.

"Hmmm?" she said without taking her eyes off what she was doing. She said it the way she does sometimes when she isn't really listening.

I swallowed hard and tried to remember my speech. I had been whispering it to myself for more than an hour, but my mind was blank. What was the matter with me? I couldn't even remember how it started. I looked at Mom. She was stirring the tea as if there were nothing more important in the world.

"Thanks," I said before she had even handed me the cup. It was the only thing I could think of to say.

She smiled and went to the refrigerator, and right before my eyes she got out the leftover spaghetti. "I haven't had any lunch yet so I think I'll warm this up," she said. "I hope the smell won't upset your stomach again."

I knew it would be torture to sit there and watch her eat spaghetti, so I grabbed a handful of crackers.

"I'll go back to my room just in case," I said.

As soon as I closed my bedroom door, my speech came bobbing back into my head. I started to go back to the kitchen to say it before I forgot it again, but the thought of that spaghetti changed my mind. Instead, I went to my desk and wrote it down as fast as I could. I folded the paper and stuffed it into my pajama pocket.

Tonight, I promised myself. At suppertime.

I must have checked that pocket sixteen times before I went into the kitchen for supper. The paper was still there.

Mom had made macaroni and cheese for me because she said that would be easy on my stomach. I tried not to eat too fast so she wouldn't get suspicious, but it sure tasted good. Even the Jello tasted good.

When I knew Mom wasn't looking, I slipped the paper with my speech on it out of my pocket and laid it on the paper napkin in my lap. I unfolded it and read it over a couple of times. This time it wouldn't matter if I forgot it. I'd have it right there in front of me.

Mom usually has a cup of coffee after supper. I decided that that would be the best time to talk to her. She's usually pretty relaxed then.

I was beginning to think Mom was going to eat all night. I don't remember her ever eating that slowly before. Finally she got up to pour herself a cup of coffee. Just as she did, the phone rang, and she went into the living room to answer it.

"Jana. It's for you," she said. "I think it's Beth."

What a time for her to call. Beth is so long-winded that I supposed Mom would already be in bed before she hung up. I wrapped my napkin around the piece of paper with my speech on it and left it in my chair.

"Hello," I said weakly. Maybe if I sounded really sick, she wouldn't talk so long.

"Jana, no matter how sick you are, don't say anything, just listen."

All I needed was another crisis. I closed my eyes and clutched the receiver, waiting for the blow to strike.

"Taffy Sinclair is up to something."

"What?" I asked.

"I don't know, but I'm sure she's up to *something*."

"Well, what did she do?"

"She didn't do anything . . . yet."

"Then how do you know that she's up to something?"

"Well, it's hard to explain."

"Try," I said. I was beginning to get a little bit tired of the whole conversation.

"It's just that all afternoon she's had this funny look on her face every time she looks at one of us. It's as if she has some secret plan, or something."

"She knows that my essay is a lie, and she's going to tell Mr. Neal!" I cried.

There was silence for a moment. "Yeah," said Beth. "That's what I was thinking, too."

I was going to be exposed. I knew it. Through the door to the kitchen I could see that Mom was clearing the supper table. She picked up the paper napkin in my chair and threw it into the wastebasket. There went my speech. But that could wait. I had more important problems now.

"What are you going to *do*?" moaned Beth.

"I don't know," I said. "Do you think she's already told him?"

"No. She's waiting. You can tell by that look on her face. She's waiting for something."

Tingles raced up and down my back. "She's waiting for me to come back to school. That's what she's waiting for. Then she's going to raise her hand and tell him out loud in front of me and the whole fifth-grade class."

There was another pause. "Yeah," said Beth again. "That's what I was thinking, too."

"Well, one thing's certain. I've got to figure out what to do by morning. I know Mom won't let me stay home another day."

"What's the matter with you, anyway?" Beth asked.

"Nothing. I just got nervous about my essay. Mom doesn't know that, though. She thinks I've got the flu or something."

"If I get any ideas, I'll call you," Beth offered.

61

"Thanks," I said. "What did the other kids think of my essay? Do you think anybody else knew it was a lie?"

"Naw. Everybody was saying how great it was. Hey, I almost forgot. All my news isn't dismal. We made enough money selling brownies to order the Milo Venus Bust Developer and give Katie back her fifty-eight cents."

"Swell," I said halfheartedly. It didn't seem quite so important now.

"I filled out the order blank as soon as I got home, and I'm going to mail it on my way to school in the morning. There's just one more thing."

"What?" I said, almost afraid to ask.

"I ordered it in your name since your mother is never home and you get the mail. We can't take any chances on our parents' finding out about it."

"Good idea," I said. At least there was something in my life to look forward to.

I hung up the phone and had just barely gotten back into bed when Mom came into my room. She had the thermometer and the Pepto Bismol again. I acted as weak and sickly as I could just in case she might decide that I needed to stay home from school for another day. I really felt like a rat faking and worrying Mom but I needed all the time I could get.

Mom looked at the thermometer and smiled. Then, as if she had read my mind, she said, "I'm sure you'll be able to go back to school tomorrow. Your temperature has stayed normal all day."

She kissed me good night and said to call her if I needed anything. Then she tiptoed out of the room and closed the door.

I was glad I wasn't very sleepy. I would have to

stay awake until I thought of a way to stop Taffy
Sinclair, even if it took all night. My mind was
blank. I got out of bed and touched my toes six
times. Maybe if I pumped some fresh blood up to
my brain it would help.

Nothing happened for a while. I was beginning
to think it hadn't worked, but then I got this great
idea. I would go to Mr. Neal myself and *confess*. I
would appeal to his sympathy. He had such kind
eyes. I knew he was a sympathetic person. I would
tell him how we were too poor to go on a vacation
and how I had spent the summer all alone in our
apartment while my mother worked to keep food on
the table. I wouldn't tell him about my father. I
would just say that I had always dreamed of going
on a two-week vacation out west and that was why I
had made up that story for my essay.

He would understand. I knew he would. And
he would feel sorry for me, and then when Taffy
Sinclair told him that my essay was a lie, he would
see her for the mean, spiteful person she really is.

It was going to be so easy that I wouldn't even
need to practice a speech, so I snuggled down into
my covers and went to sleep.

# 9

The next morning I watched Mom write a note to Mr. Neal saying that I had been absent on Wednesday because of illness, and I thought how silly some rules can be. Mr. Neal knew I had been absent because of illness. He had seen me throw up.

But rules are rules, and since I had left school the day before in too big a hurry to bring my book bag, I stuck the note in my jacket pocket along with the letter to my father and headed for school. I could hardly wait to get there and put my plan to work. I had decided to go straight to the fifth-grade room and confess to Mr. Neal before the bell rang. Taffy Sinclair was doomed.

I hurried to school as fast as I could. I only stopped once and that was to mail the letter. I even ran the last two blocks. I was huffing and puffing so hard that I was almost to the playground before I noticed who was standing beside the gate. It was Taffy Sinclair, and she seemed to be waiting for somebody. *Waiting.* That was the word Beth had used. She had said that Taffy Sinclair looked as if she were waiting for something. I had the awful feeling that it was some*body* instead of some*thing*, and that the somebody was me.

"Hello, Jana," Taffy said. She was using that icky-sweet voice that she used when she talked to Mr. Neal.

"Hi," I said. What could she possibly want to talk to me about? It could be only one thing. She was going to say she had already told Mr. Neal the truth about my essay. I could feel my ears turning red.

"That was really a super essay you wrote. I didn't realize that you had such an exciting summer."

Here it comes, I thought. The bomb. "Thanks," I mumbled, and started through the gate. I had to get out of there. I couldn't give her the satisfaction of telling me what she had done.

"Oh, by the way. I found something of yours," she said.

I stopped dead in my tracks and turned around. My heart felt as though somebody had hold of it and were squeezing it. "What?" I asked.

She waited a minute before she answered. Then she shrugged and said, "Oh, just a notebook."

I thought I'd die. There was only one notebook in the whole wide world that Taffy Sinclair would make a big deal over finding. She had found my Against Taffy Sinclair Club notebook with all the awful things about her in the front and my bust

measurements in the back. Maybe she had even sto-
len it out of my book bag while I was absent from
school.

But the worst was still to come. "I found it yesterday after you had gone home sick. I didn't know
when you'd be coming back, so I gave it to Mr. Neal
for safekeeping."

I couldn't believe what I had just heard. I
couldn't believe that anybody could do a thing like
that. Not even Taffy Sinclair. But she had done it, all
right, and she was enjoying my misery. She was just
standing there grinning. She was grinning so wide
that I could almost see her crooked bicuspid.

My knees felt as if they were going to buckle.
That would be the very last straw—if they buckled
in front of Taffy Sinclair. "Thanks," I said in a shaky
voice.

I left her standing there beside the gate with
that stupid grin on her face, and hurried toward the
school. On the front steps I stopped. What was I
doing? I couldn't go in and confess to Mr. Neal now,
not now when he had seen my Against Taffy
Sinclair Club notebook. It was bad enough that
Taffy had seen it, but Mr. Neal! How was I ever
going to face him?

I tried not to imagine Mr. Neal looking inside
my notebook, but the picture in my mind wouldn't
go away. I could just see him thanking Taffy for
being so considerate and then casually flipping
open the cover expecting to see math problems or
something like that inside. Of course he would read
it when he saw what it really was. Then he would
frown, which he hardly ever does, and think what a
dreadful person I am. And he would think that I was

jealous of Taffy because she's so pretty and that I was picking on her and being mean and spiteful.

But then he could never see her for what she really was in a million years. He was too blinded by her beauty.

The pictures kept on rolling through my brain like a runaway movie. The harder I tried to stop them, the faster they came. I held my breath as he turned to the last page, where my bust measurements were written. Surely he wouldn't laugh. Not Mr. Neal.

"Oh, Jana. There you are. I've been looking all over for you," said Beth. Her words stopped the pictures like a director calling "Cut!" "What's the matter? You look like you just saw a ghost."

"I just saw Taffy Sinclair."

"Bad, huh?"

"Worse than we thought. She found my Against Taffy Sinclair Club notebook . . . or stole it."

"What!" shrieked Beth.

"That's only half of it," I said. Then in a high-pitched voice imitating Taffy, I cooed, "I didn't know when you were coming back, so I gave it to Mr. Neal for safekeeping."

Beth was speechless, which she hardly ever is. In fact, I can't remember even one other time. She stood there with her mouth open staring at me for a full two minutes. "She *what?*"

"You heard me. What am I going to do? How am I going to face Mr. Neal?"

"How are *you* going to face Mr. Neal? How am *I* going to face Mr. Neal? How are *any of us* going to face Mr. Neal? All of our names are in that notebook!"

67

I hadn't thought of that before. All of our names were in the book. Secretly, I felt a little relieved that I wasn't completely on my own, but I couldn't say that to Beth. Besides, my bust measurements were the only ones there, and that was the most embarrassing thing of all.

"At least you didn't throw up in front of him yesterday," I said.

Beth gave me a semisympathetic look and sighed.

Just then the first bell rang. When we went in, Mr. Neal was rummaging around in the top drawer of his desk and not paying the slightest bit of attention to the students. I took a deep breath, dropped the note from my mother on the corner of his desk, and scooted to my seat.

He hadn't looked up. So far, so good. I tore a sheet of paper out of the spelling section of my spiral notebook and scrawled a quick explanation of the notebook situation on it. I handed it across the aisle to Melanie, who turned white and quivery when she read it. Christie reacted pretty much the same way. Only Katie shrugged as if it didn't matter, but after that she slouched down in her seat behind Clarence Marshall.

I couldn't look at Mr. Neal. I didn't know how I was going to get through an entire day without looking up, but I knew that I would have to try. I'd probably never be able to look at him again now that he knew such personal and private things about me. After a while my neck began to get stiff. I raised my head up far enough to look at my four friends. They were all looking down, too.

I got through the morning pretty well. He didn't call on me during history class. He called on

Taffy Sinclair. I knew why he was doing it. He was feeling sorry for her and was giving her a chance to look good in front of me and my friends. I held my breath, hoping she wouldn't know the answer. No such luck. She knew it.

As much as I was looking forward to lunch period and sitting up straight, I was dreading it, too. I knew that the spot we were in was all my fault. After all, if I hadn't thrown up and had to leave school, Taffy Sinclair wouldn't have gotten my notebook. I knew that it would serve me right if everybody was mad at me.

But if they were, they didn't say so. They just kept on asking the same question over and over, "What are we going to do?"

"We're probably worried for nothing," I said, trying to sound more confident than I felt. "Maybe he didn't even read it."

"Are you kidding?" said Katie. "Of course he read it. Teachers are the nosiest people in the world outside of parents. They read everything they can get their hands on. They're always trying to find out if their little darlings are up to something."

"Maybe he hasn't had time to look at it or maybe he's even forgotten that he had it," said Melanie. "If you ask him for it right away, maybe he'll never know what's in it."

"Ask him for it?" I shrieked, rising six inches off my chair. "I couldn't ask him for it in a million years. I'd be so embarrassed that I'd die."

"You can't just let him keep it. He might show it around to every teacher in the school," argued Beth.

"He might show it to my *mother!*" cried Christie.

I knew that she was right. After all, Christie's

mother was the principal. But all the same, I knew I could never ask him for it. I would have to stall for time until I had a better plan.

"I think we should put off doing anything until we've had more time to think about it," I said. "This afternoon is our Against Taffy Sinclair Club meeting. Let's keep thinking about it until then."

There were a lot of sour looks and some grumbles, but everybody finally agreed that we should take our time and handle this thing in just the right way. Little did I know that things would only get worse.

# 10

---

"I think Jana should sneak into the fifth-grade room during lunch period tomorrow and steal the notebook," said Katie as soon as the Against Taffy Sinclair Club meeting was called to order. "That way she won't have to ask him for it, and we'll still have it back."

"Are you crazy?" I said. "If you want it back that badly, *you* steal it."

"Jana's right," said Christie. "He would still know what was in it. And, besides, what if she got caught?"

I groaned loudly, wishing I were dead, but Beth began jumping around like a crazed chimpanzee.

"That's it!" she cried, pointing directly at Christie.

"What's it?" demanded Christie.

"You said that he would still know what was in

71

it. That's the whole problem. It's not that he has or doesn't have the notebook. It's that he knows what's in it. Right?"

I couldn't figure for the life of me what that had to do with anything, but I nodded along with everybody else.

"Don't you see?" said Beth, twirling around the room in her best theatrical fashion. "We've got to convince Mr. Neal that that notebook is a fake. We've got to make him think that there's no such thing as the Against Taffy Sinclair Club."

"Aw, come on, Beth," said Melanie. "Quit being so dramatic. How in the world are we going to do that?"

Beth grinned gleefully and then said in a whisper that we could barely hear, "We're going to be super friendly to Taffy Sinclair."

The room got so quiet that you could hear the dust settle. Everybody stared at Beth. She had to be crazy.

"I'd rather steal the notebook from Mr. Neal," I said. Instantly I was sorry I had said that, but everybody was still staring at Beth and no one seemed to notice.

We hashed it around for a while and finally decided that since no one had a better idea, the next day, Friday, would be "Be Nice to Taffy Sinclair Day." We were not only going to be nice to her, we were going to overwhelm her with kindness, and we were going to do it right in front of Mr. Neal.

Beth kept trying to reassure us by saying that we would have the whole weekend to recover from the experience. I just hoped that I wouldn't throw up on my shoes again.

The next morning I took extra pains getting

72

ready for school. If I was going to play up to Taffy Sinclair, I was going to do it on equal terms. I brushed my hair to a shine and put on a pair of yellow slacks and a multicolored sweater instead of blue jeans and a T-shirt. Then I added the finishing touch. I stuffed two cotton balls inside my training bra.

Sauntering over to the mirror, I stuck out my chest. I couldn't help giggling. I may not be Raquel Welch, I thought, but look out, Taffy Sinclair.

We had agreed to meet on the corner a block from school and to stay together as much as possible throughout the day. It was going to be grim, but at least this way no one would run the risk of having to be nice to Taffy Sinclair alone.

All the way to the rendezvous point I kept looking down at my front. I tried to do it casually so that no one on the street would notice and think that I was weird. It was funny how different I felt, even though I could still see my shoes. I could hardly wait to hear what my friends would say.

The others were all there when I got to the corner. At first nobody said anything. They all just stared. Then Katie went into her banshee routine. "Oh, no!" she cried. "What in the world do you think you're doing? Nobody is going to believe you grew those overnight." She covered her eyes with one hand and began to moan.

Knowing Katie, I hadn't expected her to be overjoyed, but she was really overdoing it. Nevertheless, I felt a blush spread up my face.

"Did you bring any extras?" asked Beth. She was so excited that I was tempted to tell her that she could have mine. Then I remembered how I had looked in the mirror, and I changed my mind.

"Naw," I said. "I didn't think of it. I'll bring some tomorrow."

Beth looked crestfallen, but before I could think of anything else to say Melanie spotted Taffy Sinclair.

"Here she comes," cried Melanie, clutching her bag of brownies like a security blanket.

Instantly Beth forgot about the cotton balls. She gathered us around her and began giving instructions.

"We don't have to be nice to her yet," I argued. "Mr. Neal's not around."

"Oh, yes, we do," said Beth. Her voice was deadly serious. "This is not going to be easy. We need all the rehearsal we can get."

Taffy was walking toward us and she was alone. When she recognized us and saw that we were waiting on the corner she hesitated for a second, but then she came on. From the look on her face you'd have thought that she was going to face a firing squad. It served her right, and I had to fight hard to hold back a giggle.

As soon as Taffy got close enough, Beth stepped forward a little. "Hi, Taffy," she said with a grin so big that it looked a little silly.

The rest of us managed weak hi's. I tried to smile, but the corners of my mouth wouldn't budge. Beth had been right. It was really going to be hard.

Taffy stopped and looked at us suspiciously. "Hello," she said. Her voice would have frozen hot lava.

"Want to walk with us?" asked Beth. Her voice didn't sound nearly as confident as it had a moment before, but she still had that stupid grin on her face.

74

Taffy didn't even answer. She just shook her head with a sort of flutter and walked on by, leaving us to stare after her like a bunch of idiots.

"Wow. Am I ever glad that nobody was around to see that," said Christie when Taffy was far enough away not to hear. "How are we going to convince Mr. Neal that we're her friends if she acts like that all day?"

Beth spun around to face the rest of us. There was a gleam in her eye. "Don't you see?" she said gleefully. "She's playing right into our hands. Mr. Neal will see how stuck up and nasty she is and how kind and friendly we are. Then he'll have to think that she faked the notebook just to make us look bad."

I wished that I could believe that, but I had the awful feeling that Beth was off on one of her tangents again. I could almost smell disaster brewing.

When we got to the school yard Taffy was nowhere to be seen, and Beth called us together for last-minute instructions. "Remember, everybody, no matter how snotty she gets, we're going to be perfectly angelic. The most important thing is to do it in front of Mr. Neal."

"I've got an idea," said Christie. "Taffy always goes into the room early because she knows that Mr. Neal will already be there and she can show off for him without anyone seeing her. Let's follow her. Then as soon as she sits down at her desk we can go in one at a time and be really friendly. Mr. Neal couldn't help but notice."

We all liked her idea. The only problem was that nobody wanted to be first. Beth thought that I should because I was president of the Against Taffy

Sinclair Club. I thought Christie should since it was
her idea. And Christie thought Beth should since
she is the best actress. Finally we took a vote. I was
elected four to one.

When we got to the fifth-grade room Mr. Neal
was already there. Taffy was there, too. She was
sitting at her desk fiddling with some papers. She
looked as prissy as ever.

I stepped in front of the open door. My ears
were getting hot and my hands were shaking. I
would rather have walked into a lion's cage.

"Go on," whispered Beth. She nudged me so
hard that I was on my way. Once I had stepped into
the room I knew there was no turning back. I swallowed hard and marched in. I went straight to Taffy's desk and stopped.

"Hi, Taffy," I said, putting everything I had
into it. Purposely I turned so that Mr. Neal could
see the big friendly smile on my face.

Taffy looked up angrily. My heart was pounding but I didn't move. The great big friendly smile
stayed on my face. I was going to make her show her
true colors if it killed me.

Then something happened that I couldn't quite
believe. Taffy started to smile. It happened so fast
that I didn't know what to do. Not only was she
smiling, but her smile was getting bigger and bigger. I could even see her crooked bicuspid. Suddenly she was laughing. My heart stopped. She was
laughing, all right, laughing and looking straight at
my front.

Out of the corner of my eye I could see that Mr.
Neal had looked up to see what was so funny. I had
an awful feeling that I knew what it was. I looked

down at my front. My worst nightmare had come true. The cotton ball on my left side had slipped down and was sticking out like a tumor just above my belt. I was so embarrassed I thought I'd die.

# 11

My life had turned into a four-letter word, which I
am not allowed to say but which kept popping into
my mind about every fifteen seconds. I spent the
rest of the day slinking around the school and not
looking at anybody. Not at my friends. Not at Taffy
Sinclair. And especially not at Mr. Neal. I was sure
that he was laughing at me and thinking how imma-
ture I was and how shapeless and ugly I was next to
Taffy Sinclair. I would have given anything to get
even with her for humiliating me like that.

When the dismissal bell rang for the day, I
pushed ahead of everybody and was the first one
out of the room. I slipped out a side door of the
building and hurried home where I could be alone.
I had to think of something to do to Taffy Sinclair. I
wanted to make her so jealous of me that she would
just about die. But how? I was the last person in the
world who could do a thing like that.

Then I got this great idea. My father should have gotten my letter by now. I was sure that when he read it and saw all the trouble he had caused and how miserable I was he would call me up long distance to apologize. He would probably say that he would do anything I wanted him to do to make it up to me. Then I would get him to give me just about the greatest present in the world, and I would watch Taffy Sinclair turn a sickly green.

The only trouble was, I didn't know what to ask for. I was too young for a car, and lots of kids have dogs. That's no big deal. But what about a horse? The more I thought about it, the better I liked the idea. I'd be the envy of the whole school. There was never a kid alive who didn't want a horse. Of course we live in an apartment, but after I had explained to him how much a horse would mean to me, maybe he would pay to have it boarded somewhere nearby.

Anyway, I was feeling so much better by the time Mom got home from work that I was actually cheerful until she reminded me that it was Wretched-Mess Day and that I hadn't even started to clean up my wretched mess.

After supper the phone rang. I nearly jumped out of my skin. I couldn't believe that my father would call so soon.

He hadn't. It was Beth calling to say that she was really sorry about what had happened with Taffy Sinclair. Then she asked me if I had any other ideas about how to get my Against Taffy Sinclair Club notebook back. I said that I didn't want to talk about it, not for a couple of days anyway. She said that she understood and we hung up. The phone didn't ring anymore that whole night.

It didn't ring Saturday morning either, and I

was starting to get jumpy. Maybe my father was in the hospital with some terrible illness and was too sick even to read my letter, much less to call me up. Or maybe he hadn't even gotten it. Maybe the mail truck that was carrying it had had an accident and was still lying at the bottom of some ravine with the driver dead, and nobody knew it was there. There were lots of things that could have happened. You read about weird things like that in the newspaper all the time. I hoped that nothing bad had happened to my father or the mail-truck driver, but deep down I didn't believe anything really had.

After lunch Mom asked if I would like to go shopping with her. She said she was going out to dinner with Pink and needed something new to wear. I enjoy shopping with Mom, and I was desperate for new sneakers, but I didn't dare leave the phone, so I said no.

After Mom left, the apartment seemed as quiet as a tomb. I couldn't remember it ever being that quiet before. It gave me a creepy feeling. Even the telephone looked about twice as big as usual. It reminded me of some monster out of a science-fiction thriller ready to jump out at me.

I decided to do my bust-developing exercises to take my mind off the telephone. When I was doing exercise number seventy-six it rang. I dived for it and answered it in just about a split second, but it was a wrong number. I sighed and went back to my exercises. My arms were getting tired, and I wanted to quit, but I couldn't think of anything else to do. Two hundred and forty five. Two hundred forty six. The telephone rang again. This time I let it ring two times while I composed myself.

"Hello," I said, trying my hardest to sound

grown up. Then I was sorry I had done that because
the lady on the other end thought I was my mother
and spent a full five minutes trying to sell me vacation property in New Hampshire before I could get
a word in.

When Mom got home she fixed me a bacon,
lettuce, and tomato sandwich for my supper and we
had a glass of Coke together while she showed me
her new dress. I was glad she had a new dress and
that she was going out with Pink even if things were
just purely platonic between them.

Every so often I would get up and go into the
living room. Then I would stare at the telephone
and concentrate on it as hard as I could, willing it to
ring, but it didn't do any good. I even thought for a
while that it might be out of order, but when I
picked up the receiver, I heard the old familiar buzz
of the dial tone.

Usually on the nights when Mom goes out with
Pink a girl named Amy Wargo comes down from one
of the apartments upstairs to stay with me. She's a
junior in high school, but she's not much fun. I've
never told Mom, but mostly she just talks to her
boyfriend on the telephone while she's here. Anyway, she came early and plopped herself down in
front of the television without much more than saying hello.

Mom took forever to get ready. I wandered
around the apartment like a zombie waiting for her
to leave.

While I was wandering around I happened to
go into the kitchen. There was Mom. I couldn't believe my eyes. She was eating a piece of salami. She
looked embarrassed when she saw me, and at first I
didn't understand. Then I remembered how she

had once told me that if a person is going to be very close to another person who had eaten onions or garlic, she should eat onions or garlic herself and she won't notice the other person's breath. I smiled to myself. Things must not be purely platonic between her and Pink anymore.

Pretty soon the doorbell rang. I knew it was Pink so I pulled open the door and stepped back really fast before he had a chance to breathe on me. I was really sorry that I'd done that, and I hoped he hadn't noticed. Pink is a nice person, and he had brought me two issues of *Mad* magazine, which is my very favorite magazine in the whole world.

After Mom and Pink left I tried to watch television with Amy, but she didn't have much to say and I couldn't sit still. About nine o'clock I excused myself and took my *Mad* magazines to my room. As soon as I closed my door I heard her dialing the telephone. It really made me angry that she was tying up the phone. What if my father tried to call?

Of course he didn't, and all I could think about was how I'd have to go to school Monday and face Mr. Neal and Taffy without my horse. I knew that I wouldn't have it by Monday even if my father called that very minute. But at least if I knew I was going to get it, I could tell everyone about it. That would be almost as good as riding it to school. I felt doomed as I crawled into bed. My father was my only hope. What would I do if he let me down again?

That Sunday was the longest day of my life. I must have looked at my watch about every three and a half seconds. I was so antsy all afternoon that I couldn't even stand still. I just kept roaming around

the apartment looking out windows and jingling my
charm bracelet until Mom said that I was driving
her up the wall and wouldn't I please sit down. I
should have known better because the minute I sat
down she started giving me the third degree about
what was wrong with me. Of course I couldn't tell
her the truth, but after about half an hour of interro-
gation I admitted that I wasn't exactly crazy about
Taffy Sinclair and that she wasn't exactly crazy
about me, either.

The minute I said that I wished I'd taken
poison instead.

"She's such a sweet girl. I don't understand
why you don't like her," said Mom.

"I just don't." I shrugged. For such a sharp person Mom sure had lousy taste when it came to kids
sometimes. She even liked drippy Clarence Marshall. There are kids that grown-ups like and kids
that other kids like, and Mom had never figured out
the difference.

"Has Taffy ever done anything to you?"

I knew that my face must be about as red as fire,
but I just couldn't tell her the truth. "No," I said.
"But you should see how she acts in school."

"Well, have you ever really talked to her and
tried to make friends?" Mom's voice was getting
stern now.

"Who wants to!"

"Honestly, Jana. You might find out she's not so
bad if you'd only give her a chance. You know,
being the prettiest girl in school can make you aw-
fully lonely. Let's face it, every one of you girls is
jealous of her whether you'll admit it or not. And if
she happens to be shy, too . . . well, maybe that's

why she acts the way she does. Maybe she's trying to cover up for not knowing how to make friends. I really think you're being unfair to her."

That was the last straw. My own mother was taking sides with Taffy Sinclair against *me* and then saying that I was jealous of *her*. I felt tears squirting into my eyes, and I ran out of the apartment, slamming the door behind me. It didn't even matter if the telephone rang. I had to get out of there. Besides, deep down I knew that my father wasn't going to call.

It was starting to get dark outside, and I sat down on the front steps for a few minutes trying to decide what to do. I could always go to one of my friend's houses, but I didn't want to do that. What I really wanted more than anything in the world was to get even with Taffy Sinclair.

Then I got this great idea. I remembered how last spring Taffy had written on the blackboard, "Jana Morgan has B.O." Well, I would get her one better.

Every tenant in our apartment building has a space in the basement to store things. I went down to our space and rummaged around until I found a can of red spray paint. Then, grinning all the way, I hurried to the school yard.

Thank goodness no one was around. I went straight to the big slab of concrete that led to the front steps of the school. I knew that I would have to hurry because it was getting dark fast. I shook the can and then began to write.

### TAFFY SINCLAIR HAS HER PERIOD

As soon as I wrote the *D* an awful feeling rushed over me. I started thinking. What if that were my name instead of hers? I'd be so embarrassed that I'd die.

I stood there until it was too dark to see the words, only I could still see them inside my head. I would have given anything if I had written them with chalk instead of paint. Then I could have washed them off. But paint wouldn't wash off even if it were light enough outside to try. Now there was nothing I could do, and in the morning everyone—Taffy Sinclair, Mr. Neal, the whole school—would see what I had done.

# 12

I tossed and turned all night thinking about what I had written on the sidewalk. I sure was sorry that I had done that, even to Taffy Sinclair. I guess I'd never realized before just how bad I really was. I had always thought that I was at least a little bit good. But now I could see the truth. I hated myself, and I kept thinking that it was no wonder that Taffy Sinclair hated me, too.

I thought about all the awful things I'd said in that letter to my father. Probably he had always known how bad I was, and that was why he had chickened out on taking me on a two-week vacation out west. He couldn't even stand to be around me. I couldn't say that I blamed him. I was probably the reason my parents got a divorce. Poor Mom. She's had to handle me alone all these years.

I knew that I could never go back to school. Taffy Sinclair would know who had written that on the sidewalk, and she would probably tell Mr. Neal,

86

who would probably tell Mrs. Winchell, the principal, who would probably call my mother. I could never go back there again, that was certain.

Then I got this great idea. There was still some red paint left in the can. Even if I couldn't wash off what I had written, I could cover it up. If I sprayed it into a solid red streak, no one would ever see those words.

I knew what I had to do. I got up as soon as it started to get light. Mom was still asleep. I got dressed and tiptoed into the kitchen. I couldn't take a chance on waking her. She'd ask a bunch of questions, and I didn't have time to think up any answers. I gulped down a glass of instant breakfast while I wrote her a note explaining that I had had to go to school extra early to catch up on some work. She probably wouldn't believe it, but I'd worry about that later.

As soon as the door to the apartment closed behind me, I peeled off down the hall and headed for the basement. I found that spray can in just about half a second and tore off in the direction of the school. I had gone three blocks before I realized that I hadn't brought my lunch. There wasn't time to go back now. It didn't even matter if I starved to death as long as I covered up those awful words.

When I got to within a block of school, I broke into a run. I couldn't get there fast enough. Then, at the school-yard gate, I stopped dead in my tracks and blinked my eyes. I couldn't believe what I was seeing. There was the custodian on his hands and knees scrubbing like crazy on the sidewalk. He must have been using turpentine or something because I could see that part of what I had written was already gone.

I jumped behind a tree before he saw me—me and my telltale can of red spray paint. He must have gotten there really early to open up the school, and when he saw what I had written he had probably decided to scrub it off before anyone else got there and saw it, too. I was so happy I thought I'd die. I loved that custodian. I'd lay down my life for him, if he wanted me to. I'd vote for him for President. I'd do anything!

My heart was pounding in my ears as I leaned against the tree. There was just one thing left for me to do. Reform. I'd never be bad again. I'd be so good that everyone in the whole wide world would love me, even Taffy Sinclair and my father. I'd start today. But first I'd have to sneak back home and get my lunch.

I pitched the can of red spray paint into a trash can on the sidewalk outside our apartment building and slipped inside, trying to be quiet as I could. When I got to our door, I put the key into the lock and turned it without a sound. So far so good. I opened the door a crack and listened. I couldn't believe my luck. Being good was already paying off. Mom was in the bathroom brushing her teeth, which meant she hadn't been to the kitchen yet or seen my note. All I had to do was get that note and sneak back to my room.

It was easy, and a few minutes later I came sauntering out as if I'd been there all the time.

The rest of the morning went pretty smoothly, and by the time the lunch bell rang I was almost starved. Katie, Beth, Christie, and Melanie and I grabbed a table in the corner of the cafeteria. There was room for eight, but we spread out our things so that no one else could sit there.

"Okay, Miss Jana Morgan, President of the Against Taffy Sinclair Club," said Beth in a very official-sounding voice. "What fantastic new plan have you devised to get back your notebook?"

For a second I thought about how I had felt when Taffy humiliated me in front of Mr. Neal, and I hated her all over again. Then I remembered what I had almost done to her. Nothing could be that bad, so I just shrugged and took a bite out of my cream-cheese-and-jelly sandwich. Besides, how could I tell them that I had reformed?

After school I hurried home where I could think. This being good was going to take planning. It wasn't something a person could just slip into like a pair of jeans, at least not someone with a record like mine.

I pitched my books on my desk and spread myself out on my bed. I lay there for ages staring up at the ceiling and trying to think of what to do. I decided that the first thing would be to write my father again and show him in my letter what a much better person I'd become. I knew that the sooner I did this, the sooner I'd start to feel better.

But what about Taffy Sinclair? I just couldn't make friends with her. That was really asking too much.

As soon as I got my stationery out, the doorbell rang. It was Mrs. Lawson, our landlady. I was really surprised to see her because she has knee trouble and hardly ever climbs the stairs. I was so surprised that I didn't notice for a minute that she was carrying a package.

"Here," she said, handing it to me. "It's for you. The mailman brought it before you got home from school."

89

It was for me all right. I took the package and looked at it, but I couldn't believe my eyes. I don't even know if I said thank you.

"Is it your birthday?" asked Mrs. Lawson.

"No," I said, feeling proud. "This is just a special present from my father."

Mrs. Lawson smiled and said something that I didn't hear and then she left. I closed the door again and took the package over to the sofa. Well, it certainly wasn't a horse. And the box was too big for a diamond ring and too small for a mink coat. But I knew it must be something valuable. Maybe he doesn't hate me after all, I thought.

My hands were shaking as I ripped the paper off. Inside was a piece of cardboard wrapped around a pink satin box. I lifted the lid and peeked inside. Chocolates. I just sat there for a while before I closed the lid. I looked for a letter, but there wasn't one. There was just a card stuck under the ribbon that said, "Love, Your Father." It wasn't even his handwriting. He must have told the candy-store people to write it for him.

I put the candy on the coffee table and went back to my room. I didn't feel like writing letters anymore, so I sprawled across my bed and listened for Mom to come home.

She couldn't believe her eyes when she saw the candy. She kept saying over and over again, "I wonder why he sent you a present. I wonder why he did this?"

I wanted to tell her, but I couldn't. Besides, I hated to spoil it for her. She seemed so happy about it. So I pretended that I was surprised, too.

The box of candy sat open but untouched on the coffee table for several days, which is strange because Mom and I are both great chocolate lovers. Finally the candy got dusty, and Mom threw it away. I was glad when it was gone. I had had a funny feeling while it was there, as if somebody had been watching me or something.

The night she threw it away I had a hard time going to sleep. I kept thinking about that box of candy and about my father and wondering if there was any chance that he was thinking about me, too. Finally I got up and dug the box out of the garbage and got the card that said, "Love, Your Father," and put it in my boot box. After that, I went to sleep.

When I called the next meeting of the Against Taffy Sinclair Club to order, I didn't ask for reports on Taffy Sinclair. I don't know why I didn't; I just didn't. Instead, I brought up something that had really been on my mind a lot the past few days: the Milo Venus Bust Developer.

"We should be getting it any day now," I said. "We've got to figure out what we're going to do with it when it comes."

"I think you should try it out first, Jana," said Melanie. "You're the president."

"Besides, it's being mailed to you," said Christie. "It's logical that you should use it first."

"Well, it was Beth's idea," I said hopefully. To be perfectly honest, I didn't really want to be the first one to try it out. After all, we didn't know that much about it. What if it was painful? Or dangerous? Maybe we would all get cancer and die. I was even sorry that Beth had sent for it in my name. What if it was six feet tall? I could never hide it from Mom then.

"Let's take a vote," said Beth. From the way

91

she said it, I could tell that she didn't want to be the first one either.

I knew that I was doomed if we took a vote, but there was nothing else to do. I was right. I was elected four to one.

Then I got this great idea. I would double my bust-developing exercises. I would triple them. I would do them every time I had a spare minute when no one was around. Surely then they would start to work, and I could say that it was all on account of the bust developer. No one would have to know that I hadn't really used it.

Deep down I knew that it wasn't going to work. Every day I did my exercises until I thought my arms would drop off, and every day my measurements stayed the same. I knew my time was running out.

I was right. Exactly three weeks from the day we ordered the Milo Venus Bust Developer, I found a note from Mrs. Lawson in the mailbox when I got home from school. She said she had another package for me. I guess she left the note so that she wouldn't have to climb the stairs again.

She must have known that it was me because she was holding the package in her hand when she opened the door. At least it wasn't six feet tall.

"My goodness, you're a popular girl these days," she said. She had a great big grin, and I tried to smile back, but my mouth was stuck.

I thanked her and took the package upstairs to our apartment. It was the bust developer, all right. The name on the return address was Milo Venus Corporation, Inc.

I took it into my room and closed the door. I

threw it onto the bed as if it were a snake. Then I just stood there for a while and looked at it. I thought about putting it in the garbage and then telling my friends that it had never come. The more I thought about that idea, the better I liked it, even though it bothered me a little bit to waste the $19.95.

It was almost time for Mom to come home, but I decided that before I threw the bust developer away I had to see at least what it looked like. I tore the paper off and opened the box.

There was a tube of cream and a book of instructions, but most of the box was taken up by a funny cone-shaped thing. I was glad that I had decided to throw it away, because I didn't like the looks of that crazy contraption.

Just then I heard Mom come into the apartment. "Jana," she shouted. "Are you home?"

"Yeah, Mom," I said. "I'll be out in a minute."

I was really glad that I'd closed my door, but I was still going to have to find someplace to stash the Milo Venus Bust Developer before Mom had a chance to see it. Just then I remembered my boot box. It was plenty big and almost empty, and what was best of all, Mom didn't even know it existed. I was pretty proud of myself for being so clever.

After supper I was sitting in the living room plotting how I was going to dispose of the bust developer when the doorbell rang. Mom was on the phone talking to Pink, so I got up and opened the door.

I nearly went into cardiac arrest. I couldn't have been more shocked if Frankenstein had been standing in the hall. I almost wished that it had been Frankenstein. But it wasn't. It was Mrs. Sinclair,

Taffy's mother, and Taffy was standing beside her with red, puffy eyes. That would have been bad enough all by itself, but worst of all, Mrs. Sinclair was breathing fire and smoke and clutching my Against Taffy Sinclair Club notebook.

# 13

Dragging Taffy by the arm, Mrs. Sinclair barged
into the room like a storm trooper. Even the fire
department wouldn't have come in like that if the
room had been in flames and Mom and I had been
lying on the floor overcome by smoke. She was huffing and puffing, and she swept right past me and
pitched my notebook onto the sofa next to Mom,
who by now had hung up the phone.

"This is the most disgusting thing I've ever
seen!" cried Mrs. Sinclair. "And I demand an instant apology from your daughter!"

Taffy threw me a terrified look, and I have to
admit that for an instant I felt sorrier for her than I
did for myself. It must be really terrible to have a
gorilla for a mother.

"Won't you please sit down, Mrs. Sinclair," said
Mom. She picked up the notebook and glanced at
the first couple of pages. When she looked back at

Mrs. Sinclair, who was still standing, she had the expression on her face that meant she was going to talk slowly because she would be thinking about every word before she said it.

"I will not sit down," Mrs. Sinclair bellowed. "And furthermore, I intend to take the matter up with the principal of the school. The idea of a club designed to torment one innocent child is something that should not be unnoticed."

I stood in the middle of the floor cringing. I was cringing so hard it felt as if I were shrinking. Five more minutes of this and I'd probably be only about two inches tall. To make matters worse, while I was cringing, my whole life was passing before me. It was all over. I knew it. My life was over, and I wouldn't even be eleven for two more months.

"Of course your daughter deserves an apology," said Mom. I couldn't believe how calm she was. "I also think that this is a good time for all of us to sit down and talk to each other and try to get to the root of the girls' problems."

I gasped out loud, and everybody looked at me. I looked at the floor. I couldn't believe that Mom would say a thing like that. How could she expect me to talk to a gorilla?

"There's nothing to talk about. Your daughter is a character assassin." Mrs. Sinclair glared at me when she said this, and I shrank another inch or two. "Someone like that on the loose can do permanent damage to shy, sensitive children like my Taffy."

Just as a picture flashed into my mind of myself locked away somewhere in a dungeon, Mom sprang to her feet.

"Just one moment, Mrs. Sinclair," she said. She

had that deadly serious tone in her voice that I knew
so well, and I was glad that she was talking to Mrs.
Sinclair instead of me. A person is powerless to resist Mom when she gets that tone of voice. "I think
you and I should go into the kitchen and discuss this
over a cup of coffee like two mature adults," she
said.

Mrs. Sinclair glared at me again, but then she
followed Mom into the kitchen just the way I knew
she would. I would have been relieved except that
on the way to the kitchen Mom gave me a look that
said, "You'd better apologize, and you'd better
make it good."

After they left the room I sat down on one end
of the sofa and Taffy sat down on the other. I don't
know if she looked at me or not, but I didn't look at
her. The room had suddenly gotten as quiet as death
except for my heart, which was ticking away inside
my chest like a time bomb.

I sat there for ages staring at the floor and trying
to think of some way to begin. Apologizing is aw-
fully hard, especially when it's not quite a hundred
per cent sincere.

While I was trying to think of something to say,
I got the shock of my life. Taffy Sinclair started talking to me.

"I didn't mean for my mother to see that
notebook," she said. "I didn't mean for anyone in
the whole wide world to see the awful things you
said about me, not *ever*. You don't know how it feels
to see things like that written down about yourself
in black and white."

Good grief, I thought angrily. Here's the
world's most conceited person and ace villain trying
to turn the tables on me. But the truth hurts.

97

I wanted to yell at her and say, "You really didn't find my notebook, did you? You stole it out of my desk after I went home sick. And you never gave it to Mr. Neal for safekeeping, either!" But suddenly it all seemed ridiculous. Taffy Sinclair and I had started out just hating each other and being snotty and stuff. Then one thing had led to another, and she had written an awful thing about me on the blackboard. She had even humiliated me in front of Mr. Neal. But then I had written an awful thing about her on the sidewalk. Now even our mothers were yelling at each other. The next thing you knew, we'd be blowing up each other's houses.

Suddenly it seemed so dumb and stupid and babyish that I didn't even want to hate her anymore. Taffy Sinclair was Taffy Sinclair, and I was me, and hating her wasn't going to change a thing. She was not the sort of person I could ever really like, but I knew that I could never really hate her anymore, either.

I felt like a creep. "I guess I don't feel so hot about having written them," I said.

I couldn't think of anything else to talk about so I looked toward the kitchen. Mom and Mrs. Sinclair were sipping their coffee and talking. They didn't look especially friendly, but at least they weren't shouting anymore. I really had never taken a good look at Mrs. Sinclair before. She was tall, and her hair was blond like Taffy's, only more of a brassy blond. I could see where she might be pretty if she ever smiled.

Taffy must have seen me looking at her mother because she said, "She's had cosmetic surgery." She said it sort of as if she were apologizing, and I couldn't help thinking how glad I was that things

like cosmetic surgery weren't important to *my* mom.
I didn't know what to say to a thing like that, so I
just said, "Oh."

The room got quiet again. I thought about what
Mom had said—that maybe it was lonely to be the
prettiest girl in school and that maybe Taffy was shy
and didn't know how to make friends, and I almost
asked her if she'd like to come over and listen to
records sometime. But I changed my mind. I really
wasn't quite ready for a thing like that.

Pretty soon Mom and Mrs. Sinclair came back
into the room. "Well, have you girls made peace?"
said Mom. Her voice sounded friendly, and we both
nodded that we had. "That's good," said Mom. "Because Mrs. Sinclair and I have decided to let you try
to work things out yourself before we do anything
like talking to the principal." I could tell by the way
she said it that Mom had done most of the deciding.

Mrs. Sinclair motioned Taffy toward the door.
Just when I was about to feel relieved that the
whole thing was over, she turned around and glared
at me again. She couldn't resist getting in the last
word. "Well, young lady, I certainly hope you've
learned a lesson from all this!" Then she went huffing out the door with Taffy in tow.

As soon as they had left I hightailed it for my
room. I knew that Mom had saved me from the
clutches of Mrs. Sinclair and had stood up for me
when she probably thought that I had done a rotten
thing. I also knew that I owed her an explanation
and a thank you, but I couldn't look her in the eye. A
little later she knocked on my bedroom door.

"Jana," she said. "Can I come in?"

It was showdown time, but what could I do?
"Sure," I said.

Mom had my Against Taffy Sinclair Club notebook in her hand when she came in. "I want to return this to you since it's yours," she said. She didn't even sound mad. I murmured thank you and reached out to take it from her. I was so shaky that I dropped it, and when it landed on my bed it opened to the page where I had recorded my bust measurements. Mom glanced down at it. I could tell by her expression that she was really puzzled.

All of a sudden I couldn't stand it anymore. Too much had happened for one day. It was as if a dam had broken somewhere inside me and all the things that I hadn't been able to talk to her about came gushing out. I told her everything. I told her about the Against Taffy Sinclair Club and the brownie sale and the Milo Venus Bust Developer. Then I told her about my essay and why I'd thrown up on my shoes and the awful letter I'd written to my father. I even told her about my boot box and all the things that I'd saved and how I knew whose fault it was that they had gotten a divorce.

When I had finished my story, I pulled out my boot box and dumped everything, Milo Venus Bust Developer and all, out on my bed, and I sat down beside it all limp and sweaty. Inside my heart it felt like the end of the world.

Mom put her arms around me the way she always did when I was hurt or sick or something. She smoothed my hair and held my face close to hers.

"You're growing up so fast," she whispered as if she couldn't believe her own words. She must have repeated that at least four times.

Any other time I might have said, "Of course. What did you expect me to do?" But this time I just shut my eyes and hugged her tight.

After we had hugged awhile Mom suggested that we go into the kitchen so she could make us each a chocolate milkshake to sip on while we talked. I nodded and followed her and watched while she put ice cream, milk, and chocolate syrup into the blender. I love chocolate milkshakes just about as much as anything I can think of, but I wasn't sure that I would be able to swallow it around the lump in my throat.

"Taffy Sinclair really is pretty, isn't she?" Mom said sort of offhandedly while she poured the shakes into two tall glasses. That really burned me up. In fact, it burned the lump right out of my throat. I had thought she was on my side.

"Well, she's got one crooked bicuspid and her mother's a gorilla!"

Instantly I was sorry I had said that, but Mom didn't seem to mind. She just sort of shrugged and said in a chirpy voice, "Nobody's perfect."

I had a feeling that there was a message for me there, but I didn't say anything. I waited for her to take a drink of her milkshake and go on talking.

"But then nobody's all bad either. I think maybe that's the solution to all your problems, Jana, or at least to most of them. You keep looking for a villain, someone to take all the blame. It just doesn't work that way—not in marriage and not among friends."

I took a long drink of my chocolate milkshake and thought about Taffy Sinclair. I had to admit that Mom had a point. But that still didn't explain why she and my father got a divorce.

"What about my father?" I challenged. "You're always telling me how great *he* is."

"He is great!" said Mom. "But as I said, everyone has faults. And when you get married, you want it to be to someone whose faults you can live with." She paused, and we both took another drink before she went on. "Your father is kind. He's gentle. He's fun to be with. He's handsome. He just doesn't take his responsibilities seriously, and that's a fault that I can't live with—not when one of those responsibilities is toward someone as special as you."

Mom squeezed my hand, and I looked down so that she wouldn't see the tears that were shooting into my eyes.

"I'm sure he means to write to you and to send your support-payment checks each month. I'm sure he even *meant* to take you on a two-week vacation out west."

The lump was back in my throat again, but there was one more thing I had to know.

"Then why didn't you tell me all this before?"

Mom blinked and looked a little sad. Then she smiled and said, "I guess I'm not perfect, either."

We finished our milkshakes and rinsed our glasses, and then Mom put an arm around my shoulder and walked me back to my room. I had forgotten all about the Milo Venus Bust Developer, and when I flipped the light switch on, it almost seemed to jump out at me from the middle of my bed. It must have seemed that way to Mom, too, because she went straight over to it and picked it up. It was really embarrassing to have a thing like that, and I could feel my ears starting to get hot.

"I'll wrap this up and mail it back for you tomorrow so that you can get your money back," she said.

I grunted an okay, but I didn't look at her. She probably thought I was some kind of nut. Instead, I started putting envelopes and stuff back into my boot box. I stood there wishing that she would leave the room before I had to look at her, but then she started talking again.

"You know, Jana, all girls don't start to develop a figure at exactly the same time. It's as if each one of us has a clock inside that's set to our own special time. When that time comes, our bodies start to change. And no matter what the advertisements claim, there's no bust developer or anything else that can make a difference before that special time comes."

Deep down I guess I had always known that what she was saying was true, but it was really good to hear somebody say it. I wasn't embarrassed anymore, and I looked up and gave her a big grin.

"You're such a worry bird!" she said as if she were scolding, but I knew that she was only pretending. "You're going to have a gorgeous figure someday."

I hoped that she was right. I had read a lot about pollution and the stuff out of spray cans, and I hoped that none of it could retard a person's development. But there I went—worrying again. I didn't want to do that so I gave Mom a kiss and said good night.

After I got in bed, I lay there for a long time thinking about all the things that Mom had explained, and I felt so much better that I thought I'd die.

The next day I called my friends together and told them that I had decided that having a club against another person was really a babyish thing. I also told them that the Milo Venus Bust Developer was a waste of time and that I was going to get our money back. To my surprise, they all seemed pretty happy about the whole thing.

I was just about to adjourn the meeting for the very last time when Katie Shannon signaled that she wanted the floor. She had a big grin on her face, and I sighed. I could almost guess what was coming next.

"I think that we should form a self-improvement club," she said importantly. "That way we can work on ways to develop into the types of young women that are needed in this changing society. And we can have more brownie sales and raise money to buy books about the women's movement and about the opportunities that are waiting for us."

Leave it to Katie, I thought as she talked on and on. Oh, well. I knew that it would be a lot more fun than hating somebody, and when she finally got around to asking for a vote, I was the first one to raise my hand.

## ABOUT THE AUTHOR

BETSY HAYNES, the daughter of a former news-woman, began scribbling poetry and short stories as soon as she learned to write. A serious writing career, however, had to wait until after her marriage and the arrival of her two children. But that early practice must have paid off, for within three months Mrs. Haynes had sold her first story. In addition to a number of magazine short stories, *The Great Mom Swap, The Great Boyfriend Trap,* and the Taffy Sinclair series, Mrs. Haynes is the author of The Fabulous Five series, which features the five best friends from the Taffy Sinclair books. She lives in Colleyville, Texas, with her husband, who is the author of a young adult novel.

Follow the adventures of Jana and the rest of **THE FABULOUS FIVE** in a new series by Betsy Haynes. It's coming in August!

Taffy Sinclair is perfectly gorgeous and totally stuck-up. Ask her rival Jana Morgan or anyone else in the sixth grade of Mark Twain Elementary. Once you meet Taffy, life will **never** be the same.

## Don't Miss Any of the Terrific Taffy Sinclair Titles from Betsy Haynes!

☐ .15413-3 **THE AGAINST TAFFY SINCLAIR CLUB** $2.50
☐ 15693 **BLACKMAILED BY TAFFY SINCLAIR** $2.75
☐ .15604-7 **TAFFY SINCLAIR AND THE MELANIE MAKEOVER** $2.50
☐ .15494-X **TAFFY SINCLAIR AND THE ROMANCE MACHINE DISASTER** $2.50
☐ .15582-2 **TAFFY SINCLAIR AND THE SECRET ADMIRER EPIDEMIC** $2.50
☐ .15557-1 **TAFFY SINCLAIR, BABY ASHLEY AND ME** $2.50
☐ .15647-7 **TAFFY SINCLAIR, QUEEN OF THE SOAPS** $2.75
☐ .15645-6 **TAFFY SINCLAIR STRIKES AGAIN** $2.75
☐ .15607-1 **THE TRUTH ABOUT TAFFY SINCLAIR** $2.75

----------------------------------------